RETURN OF THE LIVING DEAD 3

THE ORIGINAL SCREENPLAY

JOHN PENNEY

Encyclopocalypse Publications
www.encyclopocalypse.com

RETURN OF THE LIVING DEAD 3

THE ORIGINAL SCREENPLAY

INT. RESEARCH CENTER - CORRIDOR. AF-
TERNOON.

A gurney covered with a white sheet is
wheeled down a drab, industrial hallway
by TWO ORDERLIES.

Striding ahead of them are three high
ranking army officers—LIEUTENANT
COLONEL JOHN REYNOLDS, mid-forties,
walks in the middle. He is a no-non-
sense Robert Duvall type. Flanking him
on one side is a gravelly voiced,
cigar-chewing COLONEL, X early sixties.
On the other side is a pretty, but cold
looking woman LIEUTENANT COLONEL SIN-
CLAIR, early forties. Everyone speaks
with nervous anticipation.

                    COLONEL
        John, this is Lieutenant Colonel
                    Sinclair.

Reynolds and Sinclair exchange strained
smiles.

                    REYNOLDS
                    Pleasure.

                    SINCLAIR
                    Likewise.

1

COLONEL
Sinclair is here observing from
Washington. She spent two years
researching this project before
they decided to go with your
approach.

REYNOLDS
Yes I heard about your idea...
something about a steel cage?

SINCLAIR
An exoskeleton.

REYNOLDS
Oh... right.

SINCLAIR
The steel frame allowed me to
control the deceased units and at
the same time offer the mobility
to make them highly effective
bio- weapons.

Reynolds gives her a condescending
smile.

REYNOLDS
Lucky for me the Pentagon decided
on a more humane approach...

They reach a security door at the end
of the corridor.

Reynolds steps toward the door, fishes
in his pockets. He suddenly stops,
turns to the Orderly.

                    REYNOLDS
         Oh, uh... open this would you?

The Orderly takes out a silver security
card key. Reynolds smiles awkwardly—

                    REYNOLDS (cont'd)
         I… uh seem to have left my card
                    key at home.

Sinclair shoots him a dry smile—

                    SINCLAIR
         I wouldn't let it bother you.
         From what I've seen around here,
         security seems to be a rather low
                    priority.

Reynolds looks away, trying not to show
his embarrassment.

The Colonel growls bitterly—

                    COLONEL
         Damn budget chopping fools in
         congress... If it wasn't for them
         we'd have our permanent facility
                    by now.

CLOSE UP—The Orderly inserts the silver
card key. The door BUZZES open.

                                    CUT TO—

EXT. CLIFF SIDE PARKING LOT - PALOS
VERDES. LATE AFTERNOON.

An after school hang out. Teen-agers
party around their cars, listening to
music, drinking beer.

CLOSE ON JULIE WALKER.

Julie (17), sits in a beat-up old Dodge
with her group of GIRLFRIENDS. She has
a sexy, wild, unpredictable air about
her and an ever present mischievous
gleam in her dark, smoldering eyes.

Everything she wears is black—Her
leather jacket, a net top over a
leather bra, finger-less leather
gloves. Her ears are pierced with a
collection of silver earrings.

Distorted metal MUSIC blares from the
ratty car speakers, her girlfriends
CHATTER mindlessly...

But Julie is in her own world—She is
holding her hand over the flame on her
lighter, seeing how long she can stand
the pain.

One of the girls, MINDY, sees what
Julie's doing and slaps her hand
away.

> MINDY
> Julie! What are you doing? Are
> you mental?

Julie looks up, smiles privately. The
SOUND of a motorcycle approaches. The
flame flickers and blows out. Julie
looks over—

WHAT SHE SEES.

CURT REYNOLDS (17) cruises into the
parking lot on a motorcycle. He's boy-
ish-handsome with short unkempt hair;
his soulful eyes reveal a hint of something dark and lonely inside. He wears
a heavy metal t-shirt and jeans. He
gets a few looks from the crowd—He's
not quite as hip as they are, but he
tries.

> MINDY (cont'd)
> The Lone Ranger's here...

Julie scrambles out of the car, rushes
over to Curt as he pulls to a stop. She
whispers to him eagerly—

> JULIE
> Did you get it?

5

                    CURT
        I said I would, didn't I?

                    JULIE
              Let me see.

He pulls out a silver card key—with
Reynolds' picture on it, holds it up
and smiles.

                    CURT
        I helped my Dad look all over the
        house for it, but we just
        couldn't seem to find it...

                    JULIE
        Oh god Curt, this is so cool!

She laughs excitedly, throws her arms
around him. There is a beat. Their eyes
lock together... There's a real connection between them. They kiss, long and
slow. She finally pulls away.

                JULIE (cont'd)
        So how do we get on the base?

                    CURT
        No problem. I'm the boss's son,
        remember? I can do anything.

She smiles kisses him again. Mindy
calls over to them.

MINDY
Hey Julie! Are you guys gonna do
Club Kill tonight with us or
what?

Julie climbs on the back of the bike.

JULIE
I'll call you later!
(to Curt)
Did you find out anything else?

CURT
Nothing more than what we heard
him say on the phone last night.
The big test or whatever it is,
is gonna happen at six.

MINDY
Test? What test?!

JULIE
No test, Mindy. Butt out.
(back to Curt)
God it's so cruel, I bet they're
cutting up poor animals or
something... What time is it?

Curt shoots a look at his watch.

CURT
About five thirty.

7

                    JULIE
        Five thirty? Come on Boy Scout,
                we gotta jam!

Curt pops the bike in gear and they
take off.

INT. RESEARCH CENTER - ISOLATION ROOM.
NIGHT.

WE MOVE with the Orderlies as they push
the sheet covered gurney through double
air-lock doors and into an isolation
room. They hand the gurney off to a
BALLISTICS TECH and a SCIENCE TECH,
clad in protective suits.

WE DOLLY around to a strange metal
drum; stenciled across it in faded old
print is: "2-4-5 Trioxin. Property of
the U.S. Army." Through the hazy glass
portal in the barrel we see the mummi-
fied corpse of a LIVING DEAD.
WE CONTINUE around past a DOCTOR in a
protective suit to REVEAL the plexiglas
window to the adjoining observation
room. Reynolds, Sinclair and the
Colonel stand by, watching the prepa-
rations.

                   COLONEL
        Well John, let's keep our fingers
            crossed. If your preliminary

results are any indication maybe
something good'll finally come
from the Trioxin after all.

REYNOLDS
I'm sure it will, sir...

INT. OBSERVATION ROOM (LOOKING INTO
ISOLATION ROOM). NIGHT.

We are over their shoulders, looking in
at the isolation room as the SHEET on
the gurney is pulled back, REVEALING—A
YELLOWING CADAVER.

SINCLAIR
You were part of the original
team that commissioned Trioxin
from Darrow Chemical, weren't
you sir?

The Colonel takes out a new cigar.

COLONEL
Yeah, it was gonna be our weapon
in the war against marijuana
before the leak in '69 when we
found out about its special
properties... and then of
course...

He frowns as he bites off the tip of
his cigar.

                    COLONEL (cont'd)
           ...Later there was the Louisville
                  disaster in '84...
                (he spits out the tip)
           Hell, I still think we could've
           kept it all on the QT if that
           bastard hadn't made a goddamn
                  movie about it.

                                    CUT TO—

INT. ISOLATION ROOM - SERIES OF SHOTS.
NIGHT.
ON THE CADAVER'S WRISTS

A shackle is clamped around one wrist,
then the other.

ON THE CADAVER'S ANKLES. The ankles are
simultaneously shackled. WE PULL BACK
as the restraints are tightened so much
that the cadaver rises into a standing
position.

ON THE CADAVER. CLANK! A steel mouthpiece is shoved into the cadaver's
mouth, strapped securely in place.

CLOSE ON THE AMMO CASE. WHUMP! The lid
of the case is thrown open—When the
cold mist clears away WE SEE several
strange looking BULLETS packed on dry
ice. The slugs are transparent with an

iridescent blue liquid inside them. A
HAND enters frame and takes a
bullet out.

ON THE NITROGEN TANK. CLICK! A steel
mesh tube is connected to a tank of
compressed nitrogen. CLICK! The other
end is connected to a strange looking
aluminum PROTOTYPE RIFLE. WE MOVE
AROUND as the glowing bullet is put
into the steaming chamber...

                                    CUT TO-

EXT. ARMY BASE - MAIN GATE. NIGHT.

Curt and Julie drive up on the motorcycle. THE GUARD in the gate house smiles
and waves Curt through. Curt waves back
and cruises on in.

EXT. ARMY BASE - WAREHOUSE COMPLEX.
NIGHT.

Curt and Julie creep up to the door of
the large, anonymous-looking warehouse.
Black letters stenciled on the wall
read: "G-17."

                    CURT
        G-17. It's the same on the card.
            This must be it.

Curt jams the card into the key box—
Nothing happens.

> CURT (cont'd)
> Damn...

Julie grabs the card, examines it for a
second, then turns it over and slowly
LICKS the magnetic strip on the back.

She gently slips it into the slot.
CLICK! The door pops open. Julie holds
up the wet card, smiles coyly—

> JULIE
> It's all in the tongue.

She kisses him. Curt responds eagerly;
hot and intense.

Julie pulls away, whispers excitedly.

> JULIE (cont'd)
> Come on...

They slip inside.

INT. WAREHOUSE. NIGHT.

Julie and Curt come in, stop and stare
in awe.

> JULIE (cont'd)
> (whispers)

Look at all this... it's incredible...

INT. WAREHOUSE - MODEL SHOT.

Metal modular rooms have been installed in the cavernous warehouse space. The cube—like units are linked by a maze of corridors... it's like some kind of high security ant farm.

INT. WAREHOUSE. NIGHT.

They step up to the security door on the outside of the module. Curt suddenly stops Julie.

                    CURT
                 Shhh...

Curt points to the door—It's starting to open. Someone is coming out.

                    JULIE
                Oh shit...

Curt sees a ladder welded to the side of the module.

                    CURT
                 Up here.

They scramble up the ladder, duck into the shadows on top of the modules. The door slides open and an armed SENTRY

strolls out. He pauses, slips his
walkie talkie out of his belt.

                    SENTRY
              (into walkie talkie)
     Base dispatch, this is Sentry 12,
     over in the research center. I'm
     commencing my 1800 hour perimeter
                rounds now.

He strolls around a corner of the
modules.

INT. WAREHOUSE - ON TOP OF THE INCINER-
ATOR MODULE. NIGHT.

Curt and Julie are breathlessly pressed
against the smoke stack that rises from
the module and out the warehouse
ceiling.

                    JULIE
          God this turns me on...

She grabs Curt; KISSES him hard. Curt
looks down, examines the plexiglas
strips that cover the slits in the
metal roof.

                    CURT
             What's this for?

                    JULIE

14

                              Looks like they want it air
                                        tight.

                                        CURT
                              (peers through the slits)
                        Hey, check this out. We can still
                                    see inside.

INT. INCINERATOR ROOM - CURT AND
JULIE'S POV. NIGHT.

There's a stainless steel cart with
several yellow plastic bags with ''Haz-
ardous Waste" symbols on them. An OR-
DERLY in a protective suit removes a
stiff HUMAN LEG from one of the bags.

He reaches up to a lever on the chimney
where a sign reads: ''Keep flue closed
during disposal of contaminated materials." CLUNK! He throws the lever to the
''CLOSED" position and tosses the leg
into the raging fire.

INT. WAREHOUSE - ON TOP OF THE INCINER-
ATOR MODULE. NIGHT.

They both stare; repulsed and
intrigued.

                                       JULIE
                        Man, what're they doing down
                                     there?

                    CURT
              Come on.

They start away.

INT. WAREHOUSE - MODEL SHOT.

Curt and Julie can be seen scrambling
over the roof.

                              CUT TO—

INT. OBSERVATION ROOM (ISOLATION ROOM
IN BACKGROUND). NIGHT.

The DOCTOR secures sensor pads to the
cadaver's head that are connected to
an EEG monitor. He speaks into his
headset to the CHIEF SCIENTIST, a
50ish gray haired woman wearing a
headset who is in the observation
room.

The Ballistics Tech and the Science
Tech give the "thumbs up" sign; they
pull down their protective masks.

The chief scientist turns to Reynolds.

                CHIEF SCIENTIST
         We're all set here, sir.

                  REYNOLDS
         All right, let's proceed.

We PAN away and TILT UP to the vertical vent in the roof.

INT. WAREHOUSE - ABOVE THE OBSERVATION ROOM MODULE. NIGHT.

CURT and JULIE peer intently down through the vertical vent in the ceiling; the bluish-green light glows on their faces.

                    CURT
            (whispers excitedly)
        God Julie... that's my dad...

                    JULIE
        Don't worry, they can't see us.

                    CURT
        Is that guy hanging in there
                    dead?

                    JULIE
        Yeah... yeah I think so. I saw my
        uncle when he died. He looked
                just like that.

They scramble to the roof above the isolation room.

INT. ISOLATION ROOM. NIGHT.

CLOSE ON the doctor's watch; WE PAN to his clipboard as he jots down the time.

He lowers the clipboard to REVEAL the Science Tech by the Trioxin barrel. The Science Tech slowly turns a special valve on the Trioxin barrel.

There is a loud HISS as a yellowish-green mist spews from the valve. The vapor drifts down over the cadaver, enveloping it, soaking into its skin.

REVERSE ON THE WINDOW.

Reynolds, the Colonel, Sinclair... everyone watches intently, and then...

LOW ANGLE MOVING UP THE CADAVER.

After a moment we see his leg twitch... then his arm, then his eyes slowly flutter open.

INT. WAREHOUSE - ABOVE THE TEST ROOM MODULE. NIGHT.

Julie and Curt stare wide eyed at the awakening cadaver.

> JULIE
> (whispers)
> My God...

> CURT
> (stunned)
> ...It's coming back to life...

18

INT. ISOLATION ROOM. NIGHT.

JULIE AND CURT'S POV.

The cadaver's gray-yellow mouth
stretches wide around the steel mouthpiece and lets out a blood curdling
SCREAM.

The Science Tech shuts off the mist.
The cadaver struggles violently with
the leather leash-like restraints.

WHIP PAN TO THE EEG. The signal is
going crazy.

INT. THE OBSERVATION ROOM. NIGHT.

The chief scientist turns to Reynolds.

                    CHIEF SCIENTIST
          Phase one complete, sir.

Reynolds takes a deep breath, looks at
the Colonel, then back at the chief
scientist.

                    REYNOLDS
          Okay then. Proceed with the
               paretic infusion.

INT. ABOVE THE TEST ROOM MODULE. NIGHT.

Julie whispers to Curt, amazed.

                    JULIE
         Jesus Christ, it came back to
         life... I can't believe it... It
              came back to life...

INT. THE ISOLATION ROOM. NIGHT.

The Ballistics Tech raises the awkward
prototype rifle; wisps of vapor rise
off the frozen barrel.

ON THE CADAVER'S FACE. The RED LASER
sighting beam zeroes in on the cadaver's forehead as it thrashes about.

ON THE L.E.D. GAUGE. It lights up, sig-
naling when the gun is ready to fire.

CLOSE ON THE TRIGGER. The Ballistic
Tech pulls the trigger—KAPHOOMP! The
barrel FLASHES... We go into SLOW MO-
TION—CLOSE ON THE CADAVER
THWACK!

Its head jerks back on impact. The pro-
jectile is lodged in its forehead WE
PULL BACK... Small crystals of ice
rapidly form around the ears, eyes and
nose; a thin veil of frost spreads over
its skin as it freezes up.

WE PAN to the EEG—The line falls flat.

REVERSE ON THE WINDOW. WE PAN ACROSS

the Colonel, Sinclair and Reynolds as
they watch anxiously.

ON THE DOCTOR. He clicks a few
switches on the EEG, stands up,
smiles.

INT. THE OBSERVATION ROOM. NIGHT.

                    CHIEF SCIENTIST
                   (into headset)
                 Affirmative...
               (to Reynolds, smiling)
          Paralysis has been successfully
                    attained!

The room bursts into spontaneous AP-
PLAUSE—everyone smiles and congratu-
lates themselves.

INT. WAREHOUSE - ABOVE THE ISOLATION
ROOM. NIGHT.

Curt turns to Julie, a horrified look
on his face—

                    CURT
          Jesus! This is really warped! I
              can't believe my Dad—

Julie grabs Curt enthusiastically.

                    JULIE
          Oh god I know! How did they do

     it? I knew this would be worth
     checking out, I just knew it...

She KISSES him hard. The exuberant
force knocks one of her metal pins off
her jacket. It CLANGS onto the roof.

INT. WAREHOUSE - BELOW CURT AND JULIE.
NIGHT.

The Sentry suddenly looks up toward the
sound. He takes out his flashlight,
hurries over to a nearby ladder, starts
climbing.

INT. WAREHOUSE - ABOVE THE ISOLATION
ROOM. NIGHT.

The Sentry pulls himself up the last
rung of the ladder peers over the top.
CLICK! He turns on his flashlight. The
beam rakes across the modules—Julie and
Curt are gone.

                              CUT TO—

INT. WAREHOUSE - BY THE FRONT OF THE
MODULES. NIGHT.

Curt and Julie scramble down the ladder
by the front door.

Julie looks back.

                    JULIE
It's okay Curt, he didn't see us.

                    CURT
   I don't care. We're getting out
     of here, I've seen enough!

They dart to the warehouse door. He
runs the card key through the slot. The
door buzzes open. He drags her out the
door.

                              CUT TO—

INT. OBSERVATION ROOM. NIGHT.

The room is still buzzing with excite-
ment. In the BACKGROUND, the Ballistic
Tech is packing away the gun as the
doctor and the Science Tech unstrap the
cadaver, lay it back on the gurney. The
Doctor bends the cadaver's arm back and
forth, then jots a note on his
clipboard.

The Colonel chuckles happily as he
shakes Reynolds' hand.

                    COLONEL
   Congratulations John. I can just
   see it now... We'll let these bio
      units run roughshod over the
   enemy and then stroll in, freeze

                    'em up and pack 'em away until
                         the next time.

Sinclair forces a reluctant smile,
stiffly shakes Reynolds' hand.

                         SINCLAIR
            I must admit Reynolds, even
           though I think the exoskeletal
           approach would be more efficient,
               there's no arguing with your
                         results.

                         REYNOLDS
            Thank you. But it really was a
                      team effort.

                         COLONEL
            Oh don't be modest, John. This
            was your baby from the start...
             All this chummy praise is
           beginning to make Sinclair ill.

INT. ISOLATION ROOM. NIGHT.

The doctor takes out an opthalmascope,
pries back an eyelid, shines it into
the cadaver's pupil. He snaps it off,
makes another note.
In the BACKGROUND, the Colonel nudges
Sinclair and smiles proudly.

                    COLONEL (cont'd)
            John was the one who first

    figured out the poor dead
    bastards craved brains because
    they needed the electricity from
          the neurons.

The doctor pulls out a thermometer, re-
leases the steel mouthpiece from the
cadaver. The jaw springs closed. He
tries to open it—No luck. It's frozen
tight. He works his fingers under the
rubbery lips, tugs with all his might.

            SINCLAIR
        Oh, is that right?

            REYNOLDS
      Yeah well, that was a lucky
      guess. It was my team that
    discovered the Trioxin activated
    the central nervous system. Then
        it was just a matter of
    developing the acid projectiles
    that froze would freeze them up.

The Ballistics Tech walks past with the
rifle, puts it back in a carrying case.

WE MOVE IN as the doctor finally gets
the cadaver's mouth open—TIGHT ON THE
CADAVER
CRRAACK! The cadaver bites down,
crushing the doctor's fingers.

WHIP PAN to the Doctor's face. He
SCREAMS.

ON THE DOCTOR. He yanks his mangled
hand from the Cadaver's mouth.

THROUGH THE WINDOW. The plexiglas is
SPLASHED in red. Reynolds, the Colonel,
Sinclair peer at the ghastly sight in
the isolation room.

> REYNOLDS (cont'd)
> Jesus Christ. It didn't hold...
> the paralysis didn't hold!

INT. ISOLATION ROOM - ON THE CADAVER.

The cadaver's HAND reaches up, grabs
the doctor by the neck and yanks him
down.

CLOSE ON THE CADAVER'S HAND. SHUNK! The
Cadaver pierces the base of the Doc-
tor's skull with a scalpel. The doctor
SCREAMS in agony.

ON THE DOCTOR AND THE CADAVER. The Ballistics Tech dives for the cadaver,
tries to pull it off the doctor.
KAWHUMP! The cadaver knocks him away.
The Ballistics Tech panics, pulls his
gun—BOOM! BOOM! BOOM! He blasts the
cadaver.

The bullets hit the cadaver but have no
effect.

The cadaver grabs him, starts smashing
the doctor against the plexiglas. The
Science Tech frantically re—assembles
the gun.

                    SCIENCE TECH
          That won't stop him damnit! Load
               this thing up!

The Ballistics Tech rushes over,
snatches the rifle from the Science
Tech. WE PUSH IN on the rifle as a pro-
jectile is snapped into the chamber.

INT. OBSERVATION ROOM (LOOKING INTO
ISOLATION ROOM). NIGHT.

The cadaver repeatedly SLAMS the doctor's head against the plexiglas then
starts gnawing on the his neck; thick
yellow saliva dribbles down onto the
doctor's open wounds...

KAPHOOMP! The Ballistics Tech fires
from the BACKGROUND.

KASPLAT! The bullet shatters against the
plexiglas, just missing the cadaver.

INT. ISOLATION ROOM. NIGHT.

ON THE CADAVER. It lurches around, looks at the two Techs. It heaves the doctor's carcass aside and starts straight for them.

> SCIENCE TECH (cont'd)
> Again! Again!

The Ballistic Tech frantically fires again—KAPHOOMP!

THWACK! This time he hits the skull. The cadaver suddenly freezes.

UP ANGLE ON THE CADAVER. It CRASHES down on top of us.

INT. OBSERVATION ROOM. NIGHT.

The Colonel looks to Reynolds.

> COLONEL
> What the hell happened?!

Reynolds shakes his head, bewildered.

> REYNOLDS
> I... I don't know sir...
> (to the scientist)
> Strap that thing down before it
> wakes up again!

INT. ISOLATION ROOM. NIGHT.

The Ballistic Tech lowers the rifle,
stares at the carnage, stunned. The
Science Tech snaps him out of it.

> SCIENCE TECH
> (anxiously)
> Tie him up! Come on quick! Tie him up!

They drag the Cadaver onto the gurney,
start frantically strapping it down. WE
PAN AWAY from them to the Doctor—He
lies in a pool of blood and innards.

CLOSE ON THE DOCTOR'S SKULL. The Cadaver's thick yellow saliva that was left
on the wound BUBBLES and FIZZLES... The
Doctor's head suddenly jerks to life.

WE DOLLY BEHIND the Doctor as he starts
crawling toward the Techs... WE TILT UP
to the Techs as they finish strapping
the cadaver down and heave a collective
sigh of relief.

> SCIENCE TECH (cont'd)
> That oughtta keep the bastard in
> place.

He leans on the gurney; it suddenly
JERKS toward him.

> SCIENCE TECH (cont'd)
> What the hell?

He looks down, puzzled.

ON THE DOCTOR. CRUNCH! He CLAMPS his
teeth into the Science Tech's leg.

The Science Tech lets out a blood curdling SCREAM.

THROUGH THE PLEXIGLAS. Reynolds stares
in disbelief—

                    REYNOLDS
              My god no...
        (yells at the Chief Scientist)
        Contain it damnit! Seal the room
                off now!

She reaches over and pushes a panic
button. WE PULL BACK —WHOOSH! CLANG! A
steel mesh containment door SLAMS down.

The Science Tech pulls his leg free
from the Doctor.

INT. OBSERVATION ROOM. NIGHT.

                    COLONEL
        How the hell did this happen?!

                    REYNOLDS
        It's the saliva sir! The saliva!

INT. ISOLATION ROOM. NIGHT.

The Science Tech pounds desperately on the containment door as the Doctor gnaws on his ankle.

> SCIENCE TECH
> Open the door! Open the goddamn door!

WE PULL BACK and REVEAL the Ballistics Tech in the BACKGROUND. He fires —KAPHOOMP!

CLOSE ON THE DOCTOR. THWACK! He topples over, frozen.

INT. OBSERVATION ROOM. NIGHT.

Reynolds barks orders to the chief scientist.

> REYNOLD
> Send a team in there and get everyone out! I want 'em all tied down, living or dead! Keep 'em all under observation!

The Colonel chews anxiously on his cigar.

> COLONEL
> Christ John, Washington is waiting for my call. What the hell am I gonna tell them?

Sinclair steps up behind them.

                    SINCLAIR
          Don't worry Colonel, you can
               leave that to me...

WE MOVE IN on her; she gives them an
icy smile—

                    SINCLAIR (cont'd)
          Before I left, General Meade made
               me promise I'd call him
          personally... Just to give him my
               objective opinion.

WE PAN OVER—The Colonel and Reynolds
exchange worried looks.

                              CUT TO—

EXT. CURT'S HOUSE - ESTABLISHING SHOT.
NIGHT.

Heavy metal music drifts through the
quiet night air from Curt's large, con-
temporary house.

INT. CURT'S ROOM.

We are CLOSE ON a boom box. The music
plays from the small speakers. The
SOUNDS of Julie and Curt making love
can be heard coming from across the
room.

We PAN away from the boom box, past a
pair of drumsticks and a practice pad.
We discover a photo of a younger Curt
in a Boy Scout uniform next to several
Polaroids of Curt and Julie mugging for
the camera, holding up T-shirts at a
heavy metal concert.

We move off the dresser and pick up a
trail of Julie and Curt's discarded
clothes. We follow the trail across the
room as the SOUNDS of their lovemaking
reach a climax...
We TILT UP and REVEAL Curt and Julie on
the bed. Curt suddenly relaxes, gasping
for air. Julie holds him tight, kisses
his bare shoulders.

                    JULIE
     Oh God Curt it was so incredible,
                wasn't it?

                    CURT
                (breathless)
     Oh yeah... yeah it was great...

                    JULIE
                (kisses him)
     ...I wonder if he felt anything
     when that bullet smashed into his
                   skull.

                    CURT
                   What?

                                        33

                    JULIE
              (another kiss)
          That dead guy, I wonder if he
            could feel anything.

                    CURT
                  Julie...

                    JULIE
          And that scream. You remember
            that horrible scream?

                    CURT
            I'm trying not to.

                    JULIE
          Oh God I bet he was in hell... it
            must be awful to be dead...

Curt suddenly pulls away from her, sits
up on the edge of the bed, out of
breath.

                    CURT
          Come on Julie, would you give it
                a rest?

He grabs his T-shirt, pulls it on.
Julie slowly sits up.

                    JULIE
            What's wrong, Curt?

                    CURT

It's... it's just... you're so
carried away with all this...

                    JULIE
         You mean you're not?

                    CURT
Well we don't even know what we
really saw... I mean we don't
even know if that really was a
corpse to begin with. It could've
been a mental patient or someone
          in a coma...

                    JULIE
No way. That was definitely a
corpse. I told you I saw my uncle
      when he was dead.

A beat. Curt runs his hands back
through his hair. Julie can tell something's wrong.
JULIE

               JULIE (cont'd)
      You're still hung up about
         seeing your Dad there,
            aren't you?

                    CURT
Him? Oh come on, Julie... I told
you I don't care what my dad
does. I hardly ever see him
          anyway.

Julie slowly sits up next to him. She
reaches out, gently puts her arm
around him.

                    JULIE
        Good... because you don't need
            him. You've got me...

She kisses him. There is a beat. He finally smiles, pulls her back down onto
the bed.

                    CURT
        That's right, and I'm never gonna
            let you go... ever.

He holds her down, starts kissing,
groping. Julie giggles, struggling to
get free...

Car HEADLIGHTS rake across the cur-
tains above them. Curt suddenly pulls
away.

                CURT (cont'd)
                Oh shit...

He gets up, turns down the music.

                    JULIE
            What's the matter?

                    CURT
        I gotta put the card key back.

WE HEAR the front door open and close.
Julie slips out of bed, grabs her
clothes, starts frantically dressing.
There is a sharp KNOCK on the door.

                    REYNOLDS (O.S.)
                    Curtis?

                    CURT
                    Yes sir?

                    REYNOLDS
          I need to speak to you.

Curt straightens the bed, hurries to
the door, opens it. His father is on
the other side, a beleaguered look on
his face.

                    CURT
               What's going on?

Reynolds looks in at Julie then back to
Curt.

                    REYNOLDS
     I want to speak to you... Alone.
               In my office.

He turns, strides away. Curt glances
over at Julie.

                    CURT
          I think he knows something.

She gives him a worried look as he
leaves.

INT. REYNOLDS' OFFICE. NIGHT.

Reynolds pours himself a glass of
scotch, sits tiredly behind his desk.
Curt steps into the doorway.

> CURT (cont'd)
> What is it, Dad?

Reynolds takes a swig.

> REYNOLDS
> I uh... I had some bad news
> tonight...

He takes another swig, sets the glass
down hard.

> REYNOLDS (cont'd)
> ...I'm going to be re-assigned to
> another project.

> CURT
> (taken by surprise)
> What?

> REYNOLDS
> I'm being re-located to Oklahoma
> City. We report there in a week.

> CURT

(stammers anxiously)
Oklahoma City?! But Dad we... we
just got here six months ago.

REYNOLDS
(interrupts)
Look Curt, I'm sorry. I don't
like it any more than you do. But
it's nothing we haven't been
through a dozen times before.
Just have your room packed up by
Saturday. Sunday you can start on
the garage...

He yanks open his desk drawer, starts
looking through it.

REYNOLDS (cont'd)
By the way, Curt. You didn't ever
find my card key, did you?

CURT
(still reeling)
Huh? Uh no... no I didn't...

REYNOLDS
I just don't understand it, it's
got to be here someplace...

He continues to search the drawer.
After a moment, he looks back up—Curt's
still standing there.

REYNOLDS (cont'd)

39

Was there something else?

A beat. Curt gathers his nerve, speaks resolutely.

> CURT
> Dad I... I can't leave.

Reynolds just looks at him; he can't believe what he just heard.

> REYNOLDS
> What?

> CURT
> (louder, more confident)
> I said I can't leave... I don't want to leave. I finally got friends here...

Reynolds slowly closes the drawer.

> REYNOLDS
> Curtis, maybe I didn't make my self clear. I've been transferred. We're leaving in a week... both of us.

> CURT
> No dad, I'm not going.

A beat. Reynolds stiffens. He slowly rises, crosses over to Curt. Curt holds his ground.

REYNOLDS
You know Curt, I've tried to be
understanding with you lately. I
let you get that motorcycle, I
even I put up with your crazy
idea of becoming a rock and roll
drummer I because I know you're
gonna out grow it. But I've got
to draw the line here. I won't
have you defying me like this, do
you understand?

A beat. Curt remains silent.

REYNOLDS (cont'd)
And don't think I don't know
who's behind all this, either...
Moving away from that girl is
probably going to be the best
thing that ever happened to you.

Curt stares into his father's face, un-
blinking.

CURT
I'm not going.

He turns, walks away. Reynolds yells
after him.

REYNOLDS
Damnit Curtis, don't you walk
away from me when I'm talking
to you!

41

INT. CURT'S BEDROOM.

Curt goes straight for his closet,
throws open the door, grabs a backpack.

> JULIE
> What's going on?

> CURT
> My Dad's being re-assigned again.
> I told him I'm not going.

> JULIE
> You're kidding!

Reynolds storms into the doorway.

> REYNOLDS
> Curt, damn it, I'm not finished
> with you!

> CURT
> Yes you are.

> REYNOLDS
> Get back in that office!

Julie spins around.

> JULIE
> Hey, why don't you just leave him
> alone.

> REYNOLDS

          Curtis, tell your friend to stay
                 out of this.

Curt goes to his dresser, grabs his
drumsticks and some tapes, stuffs them
in the back pack.

                    CURT
          Tell her yourself... let's go
          Julie.

Julie barges through the doorway past
Reynolds. Curt is following her when
Reynolds suddenly grabs his wrist,
stops him.

                  REYNOLDS
          Goddamnit Curt, if your mother
          were alive to see this she'd—

Curt clenches his fist, his knuckles
turning white. He looks at his father
distantly, repulsed...

                    CURT
          Get your hands off me, you... you
                 freak...

Julie steps up behind Reynolds.

                   JULIE
          Come on Curt... I'm leaving...

Curt yanks his hand free and storms out

the door.

                              CUT TO—

EXT. ISOLATED COAST HIGHWAY. NIGHT.

Curt and Julie blast down the winding
coast road on his motorcycle. There is
a cliff on one side and a steep embank-
ment on the other.

EXT. MOTORCYCLE - TRAVELING. NIGHT.

Julie squeezes Curt tight, laughing,
exhilarated.

                    JULIE (cont'd)
        I can't believe you really did
      it, Curt! I can't believe it! God
            it's great! We're free!

She kisses his cheek.

                    JULIE (cont'd)
        I bet it'll be at least a week
      before my Mom notices I'm gone...

                    CURT
              Send her a postcard.

She laughs, squeezes him hard. The bike
swerves.

                    CURT (cont'd)

44

                    Take it easy Julie...

                         JULIE
                Easy? No way Curt, I'm never
                gonna take it easy on you...

She starts teasing him in a low,
vampish voice—

                    JULIE (cont'd)
                You're mine now... you hear me?
                     Mine... all mine...

Curt laughs, shrugs her off.

                         CURT
                    Come on Julie...

She bites his ear, runs her hands down
his chest... Her hand slides lower and
lower... The bike swerves erratically,
rumbles over the yellow line, shoots
toward the cliff. Curt jerks the bike
back on course.

                    CURT (cont'd)
                    Damnit Julie!

Julie laughs, excited.

                         JULIE
                What's the matter? You losing
                         control?

She kisses him again, suddenly grabs
his crotch. Curt gasps.

                    CURT
                  Julie!

The bike swerves, shoots over the
middle yellow line.

Oncoming HEADLIGHTS suddenly appear
around a corner. A horn HONKS.

CLOSE ON THE BIKE TIRE. The front end
suddenly WASHES OUT.

EXT. ISOLATED COAST HIGHWAY. NIGHT.

KABAASH! The bike CRASHES onto its side
in a dazzling shower of sparks—Curt
goes down with it. Julie is hurled
free.
CLOSE ON JULIE. She is catapulted
through the darkness.

HER POV. Heading straight for a PHONE
POLE.
ON JULIE. There is a bone numbing CRACK
as her body SLAMS into the pole.

ON CURT. KAWHUMP! The bike slides to a
stop in a cloud of dust. Curt coughs
and chokes, pulls himself off the bike.

                CURT (cont'd)

                    Julie?

No answer. Curt wipes a rivulet of
blood from his eyes, looks over.

CURT'S POV. Julie's crumpled form lies
under the telephone pole.

BACK ON CURT. He gets up, stumbles over
to her.

WE PUSH IN TIGHT ON JULIE... He reaches
out, touches her forehead. Her head
flops limply to one side, a thin
trickle of blood seeps from the corner
of her mouth.

                CURT (cont'd)
                (horrified whisper)
                Oh God no...

He shakes her gently.

                CURT (cont'd)
        Julie honey talk to me... Damnit!
              Talk to me!

He looks around, panicked, calls out
helplessly—

                CURT (cont'd)
            Help! Somebody help me!

CURT'S POV. The road is deserted.

                                            47

BACK ON CURT. He looks back at Julie,
clings to her lifeless body, tears well
in his eyes. WE PUSH IN TIGHT.

                    CURT (cont'd)
        Oh God no... please no... You
        promised... damnit Julie you
    promised... you can't leave me...
        you can't ever leave me...

A pattern of silver light suddenly
flickers onto his face.

He slowly looks down.

ON THE GROUND. The light is glinting
off—THE SILVER CARD KEY that has
slipped out of his pocket.

TIGHT ON CURT. He slowly picks up the
card key. WE MOVE UP... There is a
beat... A dark, twisted idea is born...

                                    CUT TO—

EXT. ARMY BASE - MAIN GATE. NIGHT.

Curt drives with grim determination up
to the army base.

Julie's head lies limply against his
shoulder; her arms are around his waist
with her wrists tied together. Curt
waves at the guard as he cruises in.

ON THE GUARD. He looks curiously after Curt for a moment, then shrugs it off.

INT. WAREHOUSE. NIGHT.

Curt has Julie draped over his shoulder in a fireman's hold. He fumbles nervously with the card key, finally manages to slide it into the lock. The door to the modules buzzes open.

INT. RESEARCH CENTER - CORRIDOR. NIGHT.

He creeps down the shadowy corridor, struggling under Julie's weight. The place is quiet, deserted. He is almost to the observation room when the sound of heavy FOOTSTEPS suddenly echo from around the corner. Curt looks around frantically, ducks behind a containment door frame just as the SENTRY comes around the corner and heads the other way.

ON CURT AND JULIE. Curt squeezes up against the wall. He looks over, peers through the slats and sees—

CURT'S POV - AN ADJOINING ROOM. SINCLAIR is furtively working on A SEVERED HUMAN ARM. It's alive, twitching spasmodically. She drills a hole through the fore arm, then threads a steel bolt

49

through it, fastening it to some sort
of metal jointed frame.

BACK ON CURT AND JULIE. Curt stifles a
horrified gasp. Julie's limp hand
slips, BUMPS against the metal wall.

CURT'S POV - AN ADJOINING ROOM. Sinclair gets up, comes toward us. She
peers out through the slats.

ON CURT AND JULIE. Curt scrunches back
against the wall, holding his breath...
ON SINCLAIR. She finally turns, heads
back to her work.

ON CURT AND JULIE. Once the coast is
clear, he hefts Julie's body back over
his shoulder and crosses to the observation room door. He slips the card key
in the lock.

INT. OBSERVATION ROOM - LOOKING INTO
AIR LOCK. NIGHT.

He crosses the dark room, pulls open
the air lock door and goes through the
chamber. WE PAN with them...

He lays Julie gently on the floor in
the middle of the isolation room,
crosses to a rack where several protective suits are hanging. He grabs one.

INT. CORRIDOR. NIGHT.

The Sentry continues on his rounds.

                              CUT TO—

INT. ISOLATION ROOM. NIGHT.

Curt zips up the suit, pulls the mask
down over his face.

He looks over at the Trioxin barrel
that was used in the experiment. WE
MOVE IN on the barrel—The ghastly, mum-
mified corpse peers out.

Curt wheels the barrel over next to
Julie.
CLOSE ON THE BARREL VALVE. Curt tries
to turn the special valve that has been
installed on top—Nothing happens. He
turns it some more, taps it. Nothing.
It's been disconnected.

WE TILT UP to Curt—

                    CURT
               Damn...

He grabs a surgical instrument, digs it
along the seam of the glass portal...
He grimaces, leans into it—CRACK! The
glass shatters. WHOOOOSH! The yellow-

ish-green mist BLASTS out, knocking him off his feet.

He crashes against the plexiglas window.

                                    CUT TO—

INT. CORRIDOR. NIGHT.

The Sentry stops, thinks he hears some-thing. He waits for a moment, then con-tinues on his way.

                                    CUT TO—

INT. ISOLATION ROOM. NIGHT.

Curt scrambles to his feet, crosses past the barrel.

WE MOVE IN on the shattered glass portal.

ON CURT AND JULIE. Curt kneels by Julie. The mist swirls around her body, soaking into her skin.

                    CURT (cont'd)
                    (whispers)
          Oh God... I hope you were
        right... I hope this really does
                    work...
                    (nervous)

> Well you see... you... when we
> were on the bike...

Before he can say another word, there
is a loud CLANG! They both flinch.

> JULIE
> What was that?

They get up, look over at the isolation
room.

> CURT
> Oh no...

THROUGH THE PLEXIGLAS, we see the
barrel lying on its side, black sludge
oozes out—It's empty.

ON CURT AND JULIE. Curt starts frantically peeling off his protective suit.

> CURT (cont'd)
> Let's get the hell out of here...

> JULIE
> What's going on, Curt?

Curt takes her hand. They start past
the air lock chamber, suddenly—The
hideous barrel CORPSE lurches out at
them.

Its blistery jaw stretches open re-

53

vealing its green-black throat. It lets out a guttural, vomitous SCREECH!

> JULIE (cont'd)
> What the fuck is that?!

Curt SLAMS the air lock door on the corpse, spins the wheel lock. The corpse WAILS in pain, pounds on the window in the door.

> CUT TO—

INT. CORRIDOR. NIGHT.

The Sentry hears something, turns and heads back the other way.

ON JULIE'S HAND. Her finger twitches. Curt looks down.

> CURT
> Julie!

She stirs groggily. He gathers her in his arms, takes her to the air lock doors.

INT. OBSERVATION ROOM.

He comes in, lays her on the floor, yanks off his protective mask. Julie's eyes flutter open. She suddenly inhales sharply.

54

                    JULIE
                 (exhilarated)
             Oh God Curt, that was
             incredible... let's do it
                    again...

She grabs Curt, pulls him down on top
of her, kisses him passionately. All of
a sudden she stops.

                 JULIE (cont'd)
                  (puzzled)
             What is this? What are you
                   wearing?

                    CURT
             You don't remember?

                    JULIE
             Remember what? wait a minute...
             how did we get here?

She looks around, dazed, then suddenly
looks down at her finger tips, taps
them gently.

                 JULIE (cont'd)
             I'm so numb...

She rubs her neck.

                 JULIE (cont'd)
             And my neck... it hurts...

                                              55

She starts to sit up—Her head jerks
back and forth erratically.

> JULIE (cont'd)
> What's going on? What's wrong
> with me?

INT. OBSERVATION ROOM. NIGHT.

Curt and Julie scramble toward the
door. He searches his pockets, takes
out the card key. Julie looks over her
shoulder, panicked.

> JULIE (cont'd)
> Hurry!

ON THE BARREL CORPSE. It pounds at the
air lock door window.

BACK ON JULIE AND CURT. Julie's wobbly
legs suddenly give out. Curt catches
her, helps her up. She looks down at
her limp legs.

> JULIE (cont'd)
> My god, what's wrong with me?

She clutches her chest.

> JULIE (cont'd)
> I... I can't feel my heart
> beating...
> (panicked)

I can't feel my heart!

Curt inserts the card key. It doesn't work.

                    CURT
          Damnit! It's not working!

He starts frantically jamming and re-jamming the card in the lock.

                    JULIE
          Tell me what's going on... What
               happened to me?

In the BACKGROUND WE SEE the wheel lock slowly start to turn... The barrel corpse has figured out how to get out...

                    CURT
          You had an accident.

                    JULIE
          What kind of accident?

                    CURT
          On the bike.

                    JULIE
          What happened?

                    CURT
          You died...

Julie staggers back, next to the air
lock door.

                    JULIE
                  (stunned)
                 I WHAT?!

                    CURT
        You died... I brought you here
                    and...

CALANG! The air lock door suddenly
BURSTS open. The Barrel Corpse lunges
out at Julie. Curt leaps over, body
slams the corpse. It CRASHES into the
supply shelves.

                                    CUT TO—

INT. CORRIDOR. NIGHT.

The Sentry starts running down the hall
toward the SOUNDS.

                                    CUT TO—

INT. OBSERVATION ROOM. NIGHT.

They race to the door. Curt desperately
licks the card, inserts it. It works.
The Barrel Corpse SCREECHES behind
them. They look back—

ON THE BARREL CORPSE. It tears its face

away from its shoulder, peeling away
its rotting skin. It starts coming toward them.
Curt and Julie dart out the door.

INT. CORRIDOR. NIGHT.

Curt drags Julie down the hall to the
exit door. The Sentry rushes out behind
them, draws his gun.

> SENTRY
> Halt!

ON THE SENTRY. He is about to fire when
—The corpse LEAPS out, grabs him by the
neck, SMASHES his head against the
metal wall, turns him over —CARRUNCH!
It RIPS open the base of the Sentry's
shattered skull. An ALARM starts to
blare through out the complex.

RAPID DOLLY IN ON JULIE. She stares
horrified at the hideous corpse ripping
the Sentry's skull apart.

> JULIE
> Oh God Curt... Is that what I'm
> going to become?

Curt grabs her by the arm, drags her
out the door.

EXT. ARMY BASE - WAREHOUSE COMPLEX.
NIGHT.

Curt races to his bike. Julie stumbles
after him in a daze.

                    CURT
              Julie come on!

He helps her on the back, fires it up,
screeches away just as 2 MPS rush toward them.

EXT. ARMY BASE - MAIN GATE. NIGHT.

Curt blasts past the gate house on the
bike. The guard jumps out after them.

                              CUT TO—

INT. CORRIDOR. NIGHT.

CLOSE ON THE CORPSE. It SCREECHES mis-
erably, blood and innards spilling out
of its green-black mouth.

WE TILT UP to a CLOSE CIRCUIT SUR-
VEILLANCE CAMERA on the wall.

                              CUT TO—

INT. CORRIDOR - A GRAINY BLACK AND
WHITE VIDEO IMAGE. NIGHT.

The tortured corpse is in its feeding frenzy, HOWLING, feasting on the Sentry's brain.

The image CUTS TO—JULIE and CURT coming in the door backwards. The scene plays in REVERSE MOTION as they re—witness the Sentry's death.

                    COLONEL (O.S.)
          It's him all right...

INT. OBSERVATION ROOM. NIGHT.

Reynolds stares in silent horror at the TV MONITOR re-playing the scene. The Colonel and the chief scientist are hunched over Reynolds' shoulder.

                    COLONEL (cont'd)
          Looks like we found your card.

                    REYNOLDS
          (whispers to himself)
          Jesus Curt... what have you done?

                    COLONEL
          I put a state wide APB out on your
          son's motorcycle. As far as the
          cops are concerned, we're after
          them for possession of government
          property. I'm also having the
          containment squad assembled now.

INT. CORRIDOR - VIDEO IMAGE. NIGHT.

Reynold's finger enters frame—CLICK! He
FREEZE FRAMES the playback tape on a
CLOSE SHOT of CURT.

INT. OBSERVATION ROOM. NIGHT.

Reynolds slowly looks up, speaks quietly to the Chief Scientist.

> REYNOLDS
> You're sure his girlfriend's
> dead?

> CHIEF SCIENTIST
> I reviewed the automated security
> tapes of the isolation room.
> That appears to be the
> case, yes.

A beat. Reynolds takes a moment to ab-
sorb this, then—

> REYNOLDS
> So what are his chances? What are
> my son's chances?

> CHIEF SCIENTIST
> Well, it depends on how soon we
> can get to him.

> REYNOLDS
> What do you mean?

CHIEF SCIENTIST
From what I can tell, it seems
his girlfriend was brought back
completely intact, she's still
got a brain and there's also
obviously a strong connection
between them... that should be
enough to keep her from attacking
him... at least...

She looks up at Reynolds, slowly takes
off her glasses.

CHIEF SCIENTIST (cont'd)
At least for a few hours until
her brain begins to decay
naturally and shut down... and
then it's a different story... if
she attacks him, and her saliva
comes in contact with any part of
his exposed nervous system... he
could become like her...

The news hits Reynolds' hard. He looks
grimly back at the TV. Sinclair breezes
crisply into the room, urgently ad-
dresses the Colonel.

SINCLAIR
Pentagon Special Command will be
here in six hours. They're
leaving Washington now.

COLONEL

63

                    Thank you, colonel

A beat. Sinclair looks over at Reynolds
who continues to stare forlornly at the
playback screen.

                        SINCLAIR
             Sir... I suggested to General
             Meade that I go ahead and take
             over science operations now.

                        COLONEL
             Your command doesn't start here
                  until 0900 tomorrow.

                        SINCLAIR
             I know sir... but given the
                  circumstances...

She nods in Reynolds' directions. The
Colonel considers this for a moment,
then shakes his head.

                        COLONEL
             No. Command will stand with
             Reynolds until they arrive.

Sinclair fumes...

                                      CUT TO—

EXT. DOWNTOWN - CITY STREET. NIGHT.

Curt and Julie travel down a dark inner

city street on his bike.

EXT. MOTORCYCLE - CITY STREET.
NIGHT.

Curt drives intently. Julie's in the
throes of an anxiety attack, frantically touching her face—

                    JULIE
        Oh Jesus Curt, am I dead? Am I
        really dead? my skin... it feels
                    funny...

She smells her hand, then her arm.

                    JULIE (cont'd)
        Do I smell? I don't smell do I?

                    CURT
                You smell fine.

She anxiously clutches Curt.

                    JULIE
        Oh god Curt I'm so hungry. If I
        could just get something to eat
                I'll be okay...

                    CURT
        I'm working on it Julie, I'm
        trying to find something open.

                    JULIE

                    I saw a mall back there, why
                    don't we go back and—

                              CURT
                    Too crowded. They're gonna be
                    looking for us.

Julie suddenly grabs Curt's arm, her
eyes filled with anger; she's not
screwing around anymore—

                              JULIE
                    Curt! Get me some fucking
                    food! Now!

                                        CUT TO—

EXT. DOWNTOWN LIQUOR STORE. NIGHT.

A small corner store with barred
windows in a rough looking neighbor-
hood. Julie and Curt pull up on the
bike.

INT. LIQUOR STORE. NIGHT.

The Korean STORE OWNER is behind the
counter, warily watching a motley group
hanging around the video game.

The big burly one is ARTURO "SCRATCH"
MACHADO, early thirties. Next to him is
MOGO, fifteen, intently playing the
video game.

Scratch's girlfriend, ALICIA, eighteen, trashed-out, sexy, hangs on Scratch's shoulder. The other one is FELIPE, twenties, a hyped up Scratch wanna-be. He sits next to their boom box restlessly eating a chocolate bar.

Scratch urges Mogo on.

                    SCRATCH
        That's right, kill 'em... kill
        'em all... now grab the shit and
                get out of there!

Distorted gunfire roars over the ratty game speakers.

                    MOGO
            Die motherfuckers!

Alicia purrs in Scratch's ear.

                    ALICIA
        Let's get out of here Santo, I'm
                    bored...

                    SCRATCH
        Just a few more minutes...

                    ALICIA
        You said that an hour ago.

                    FELIPE
        Hey man, if we left when you

wanted to, he'd never've gotten
to level seven.

ALICIA
What's the big deal? It's just a
stupid fucking video game.

Alicia sighs, crosses her arms and
slumps against the machine.

INT. ACROSS THE STORE. NIGHT.

Julie and Curt come into the store.
Scratch and Felipe give them a long
look as Julie makes a bee line to the
junk food rack. She starts grabbing
everything she can—Doritos, Ding Dongs,
Twinkies...

Curt snatches the Doritos from her—

CURT
You don't need all this.

She snatches it back from Curt.

JULIE
Leave me alone. I don't know what
I want yet.

CURT
Well when're you gonna know?

She eyes the food like a hungry animal.

68

                    JULIE
              When I taste it.

She grabs more junk food. Scratch walks
over.

                   SCRATCH
         Hey man, what the fuck's wrong
               with her?

                    CURT
                (distracted)
         Nothing. She's fine.

                   SCRATCH
         Hey don't you ever feed her?

Curt tries to wrestle the Ding Dongs
away. She jerks them back.

                    CURT
                 (fuming)
              Julie!

                   FELIPE
         Hey, the man asked you a fucking
               question...

Curt spins around, accidentally bumps
into Scratch.

                    CURT
              (snaps angrily)
         Hey, just stay out of this, will

                    you?!

Felipe looks at Scratch, surprised.

                   SCRATCH
          What did you say to me?

Curt looks up at the massive man.

                    CURT
       Listen... I... I don't want any
               trouble, I...

Julie is oblivious to the confronta-
tion. She starts tearing open the pack-
ages, stuffing the junk food in her
mouth.

Curt and Scratch remain squared off.

                 CURT (cont'd)
          Look whatever I said, I'm
               sorry... I...

                   FELIPE
       Sorry isn't good enough, fly
       ball. No one does that to Santo
          and gets away with it...

                    CURT
       It was an accident, I didn't
       know you were right behind me.
          Now would you please just
                 let us—

A frantic VOICE suddenly interrupts
them.

> STORE OWNER (O.S.)
> Hey!

They look over and see the Korean store
owner rushing toward them.

> STORE OWNER (cont'd)
> Hey you buy that first then you
> eat it!

ON JULIE. She is on the floor now,
amidst a pile of half eaten junk food.
She stuffs a handful of Twinkies into
her mouth, makes a face, spits it out,
tries Ding Dongs.

The store owner gathers up the un-
opened food, putting it back on the
shelf.

> STORE OWNER (cont'd)
> You pay me and get out!

Curt reaches into his pocket, takes out
his wallet.

> CURT
> Yeah, yeah take it easy... we
> will... here...

AT THE VIDEO GAME. Mogo looks up and

SEES: The unattended cash register across the store. He looks over at the store owner YELLING and putting the food away.

He darts over behind the counter, starts punching the keys on the register. DING! The drawer pops open.

ON THE STORE OWNER. He sees Mogo behind the counter, drops the food.

> STORE OWNER
> Hey get out of there!

He starts toward the register. Scratch blocks his way, Felipe swoops up behind him. The store owner is surrounded.

He panics, reaches behind his back, pulls a PISTOL from his belt, steps back and aims at both of them.

> STORE OWNER (cont'd)
> Out of my way!

Scratch and Felipe freeze. The store owner rushes past them.

AT THE COUNTER. Mogo darts away from the register with a fistful of cash.

> STORE OWNER (cont'd)
> Drop it!

The store owner takes aim. Scratch
knocks his arm. BOOM!

KABAASH! The stray bullet shatters the
front window. An ALARM starts to RING.

Scratch and the Store Owner struggle
for control of the gun. BOOM! There is
a muffled shot.

Alicia looks down at the wounded store
owner, gasping for air, clutching his
stomach.

                    ALICIA
        My god Santo! What the hell did
                   you do?!

Scratch leaps off him, taking the
pistol with him.

                   SCRATCH
        Let's just get the fuck out of
                    here!

Felipe cackles excitedly, a wild look
in his eyes; he brutally KICKS the
store owner.

                    FELIPE
        Hey look Santo, he bleeds man!

                   SCRATCH
           Mogo, let's go!

Mogo SLAMS into Julie on his way to them.

                    MOGO
          Out of my way, bitch!

WHUMP! He shoves her out of the way. She strikes back, baring her teeth—CAR-RUNCH! She bites his arm.

                    MOGO (cont'd)
                    AYYE!

WHAP! He slaps her and dodges out the door after Scratch, Alicia and Felipe.

EXT. LIQUOR STORE. NIGHT.

Mogo follows Scratch, Alicia and Felipe toward SCRATCH'S CAR. BOOM! Scratch rips off a shot, hitting the front tire of Curt's bike. They jump into their car and they peel out.

INT. LIQUOR STORE. NIGHT.

Julie wipes her bloody mouth... Something about Mogo's flesh tastes good... she tastes it again.

The ALARM continues to BLARE. Curt pulls her to her feet.

                    CURT

> Come on, we got to get out of
> here before the cops come!

He pulls Julie out the door.

EXT. LIQUOR STORE. NIGHT.

Curt and Julie run over to his bike;
they see the flat tire.

> CURT (cont'd)
> Shit!

He looks over at the liquor store DE-
LIVERY VAN, parked nearby.

> CURT (cont'd)
> Come on.

He drags Julie to the van, climbs in.

INT. DELIVERY VAN. NIGHT.

Curt slides behind the wheel, slams the
door.

> CURT (cont'd)
> Keys! I need keys!

He flips down the visor, checks under
the mat, searching frantically.

WHUMP! The STORE OWNER suddenly appears
at the side window, holding the keys.

                    STORE OWNER
                  (winces painfully)
          Help me... The hospital... it's
               only two blocks...

                      CURT
          All right... all right... get in!

Curt snatches the keys. The store owner
climbs in the side door. Curt turns the
ignition; the engine struggles to
catch.

EXT. STREET OUTSIDE THE LIQUOR STORE.
NIGHT.

A COP CAR screeches up. A COP gets out,
races up to the side window of the van
with his gun drawn.

                      COP
                    Freeze!

Curt starts the van, punches it. The
van takes off.

INT. DELIVERY VAN. NIGHT.

The store owner looks around, panicked.

                   STORE OWNER
          Stop... Stop... I'll go with
            them... I'll go with the
                 police...

BOOM! A gunshot rings out behind them.
Julie SCREAMS, ducks.

                    CURT
          They're shooting at us! Jesus
          Christ they're shooting at us!

Curt slams the peddle the metal. The
van jerks forward; the store owner topples back.

                                    CUT TO—

INT. RESEARCH CENTER - CORRIDOR. NIGHT.

An MP races down the hall to Reynolds'
office.

INT. REYNOLDS' OFFICE. NIGHT.

The MP rushes in, Reynolds looks up
from behind his desk.

                    MP
          The police found your son, sir.

Reynolds leaps up, grabs his coat.

                    REYNOLDS
               Where?!

                    MP
          South Central. They're in pursuit
               now!

They dash out.

                                    CUT TO—

EXT. ARMY BASE - MAIN GATE. NIGHT.

The specially outfitted Containment
Squad ARMY TRUCK roars out of the gate.

                                    CUT TO—

EXT. CITY STREET. NIGHT.

The van speeds down the street, the cop
car in hot pursuit.

INT. DELIVERY VAN - HIGH SPEED.

ON JULIE'S HAND She clutches one of the
silver pins from her jacket and is ab-
sent-mindedly STICKING the back of her
hand with the sharp point. WE TILT UP
to Julie and Curt...

                    JULIE
          Oh God Curt... I'm hungry...

                    CURT
          You're WHAT?

                    JULIE
          I'm still hungry Curt... I'm
                  starving...

BOOM! KABASH! The rear window is suddenly SHATTERED.

> CURT
> For Christ's sake Julie how can
> you think of food at a time like
> this!

The store owner clambers for the back door.

> STORE OWNER
> Stop... I... I want out...

He throws open the back door, waves frantically—

> STORE OWNER (cont'd)
> Don't shoot! Don't—

BOOM ! KATHWACK! A bullet SMASHES into his head, tearing open his skull. He crumples forward, hits the floor DEAD.

Curt looks in the mirror, horrified—

> CURT
> Shit! They killed him!

Julie leaps out of her seat.

> CURT (cont'd)
> No Julie! Stay down!

79

It's too late, she's already on
her way.

EXT. SIDE STREET/DEAD END ALLEY - DOWN-
TOWN. NIGHT.

The van turns off the side street and
into the alley.

EXT. DEAD END ALLEY. NIGHT.

THROUGH A CHAIN-LINK FENCE (LOOKING OUT
THE ALLEY). The van races toward us;
the headlights snap off. It comes right
up to us and suddenly SLAMS on its
brakes—WE RACK FOCUS to the fence in
the foreground.

                    CURT
            Damnit! Dead end!

WE RACK FOCUS as the COP CAR races past
the alley entrance without turning in.

INT. DELIVERY VAN. NIGHT.

Curt sighs, closes his eyes.

                CURT (cont'd)
            Thank god... I think we lost
                    'em...

There is a moment of silence and then a
strange SQUISHING SOUND starts to come

from the darkness in the back of
the van.

> CURT (cont'd)
> Julie?

No answer.

> CURT (cont'd)
> Julie... What's that noise?

The SLURPING sounds grow louder. Curt
turns around, squints into the back of
the van.

CURT'S POV. Julie is stooped over the
dead store owner, slurping up his
brain.

Curt gags, stunned—

> CURT (cont'd)
> Jesus Christ WHAT ARE YOU DOING?!

EXT. SIDE STREET/DEAD END ALLEY.
NIGHT.

The cop car comes down the street,
screeches to a stop in front of the
alley.

INT. DELIVERY VAN. NIGHT.

Curt leaps into the back of the van. He

grabs Julie's arm, starts pulling her away from the store owner's body.

                    CURT (cont'd)
               Stop it! Stop it!

She shoves him away, continues to feed in a frenzy. WHAP!

He slaps her out of it, drags her OUT OF FRAME.

                                   CUT TO—

EXT. DEAD END ALLEY. NIGHT.

The cop car turns into the alley, cruises slowly toward us, comes to a stop behind the van. The doors open; two COPS come out with their guns drawn. COP #1 exits FRAME; Cop #2 approaches the van; it rocks slightly.

INT. VAN - LOOKING OUT DRIVER'S SIDE WINDOW. NIGHT.

Cop #1 moves past the window, looking into the dark interior.

                    COP #1
     We know you're in there! Come out
          slowly with your hands up!

EXT. DEAD END ALLEY. NIGHT.

Cop #1 gives the signal to Cop #2. Cop #2 slowly starts for the rear doors of the van.

> COP #1 (cont'd)
> This is your last warning... come out or we're coming in after you!

EXT. DEAD END ALLEY. NIGHT.

Cop #2 goes up to the rear doors of the van, reaches out for the handle... KAWHUMP! The door suddenly BURSTS open—

The STORE OWNER'S bloody corpse lunges out; the top of his head is missing from his eyebrows up. He wields a heavy tire iron.
CRACK! The Store Owner pierces the tire iron through the cop's eye and out the back of his skull. BOOM! BOOM! BOOM!

The cop jerks spasmodically, firing off his pistol.

ON COP #1. He hurries around the van with his gun poised and SEES—

COP #1'S POV. The store owner CRACKING open the cop's skull with the tire iron and picking out the brains like he was eating a crab delicacy.

ON COP #1. He opens fire in a blind
panic—BOOM! BOOM! BOOM!

ON THE STORE OWNER. The bullets SLAM
into the store owner but have little
effect. He lurches to his feet and
starts toward the cop.

Cop #1 backs against the van.

BEHIND THEM. A COP CAR and the ARMY
TRUCK screech to a stop at the entrance
of the alley. WHUMP! The rear door
flies open. The specially outfitted
CONTAINMENT SQUAD soldiers leap out.

BACK ON COP #1. The Store Owner swings
the tire iron—WHOOSH CLANG! It hits the
van door, missing Cop #1. He raises the
tire iron again, about to strike—
KAPHOOMP! THWACK! The Store Owner stops
short, falls out of frame.

LOOKING OUT THE ALLEY. The containment
squad members rush down the alley,
Reynolds with them. Cop #1 stares down
at the Store Owner on the ground,
stunned.

Reynolds looks around as the dead end
alley. The SQUAD LEADER strides up
to him.

                    SQUAD LEADER

No sign of your son or the
girl, sir.

REYNOLDS
Damnit... All right. We'll make
this our starting point. Begin a
360 sweep search. Keep widening
the pattern out until we find
them. And remember no matter
what, don't harm the boy!

SQUAD LEADER
Yessir.

The Squad Leader exits. Reynolds looks
up, searching the dead end alley...

WE TILT DOWN to a STORM DRAIN OPENING
in the shadows... The cover settles
into place...

CUT TO—

INT. VIADUCT. NIGHT.

WE FOLLOW Curt and Julie out of the
blackness and into the shadowy viaduct
under a bridge that spans the L.A.
river.

They stagger to a stop on opposite
sides of the cement passageway.

Curt leans against a grimy wall,
clutching his stomach.

> CURT
> Oh God... this can't be
> happening... this can't be
> happening...

He suddenly doubles over, starts
throwing up.

ON JULIE. Tears stream down her cheeks
as she POUNDS her head against the wall
like a frustrated child.

> JULIE
> I'm sorry... I'm sorry... I'm
> sorry... I'm sorry...

BACK ON CURT. Julie continues her
mantra off screen as Curt whispers desperately.

> CURT
> (whispers desperately)
> God... Oh God this's got to be a
> nightmare...

Julie suddenly CRIES OUT in pain.

WE FOLLOW Curt as he goes over to
Julie. She is shivering, twisting her
hand back and forth, doing something to
her arm.

                    JULIE
          It... it's started again...

WE TILT DOWN and REVEAL that she is
anxiously twisting an old rusty spring
into her arm. It gouges deeper and
deeper into her flesh...

                    CURT
                 (repulsed)
          What're you doing to yourself?!
                  Stop it!

He tries to stop her. WHAP! She SLAPS
his hand away.

                    JULIE
          Don't touch me! Stay away
                from me!

Curt steps away from her, repulsed.

                    CURT
          What's happening to you? How
          could you do it, Julie? How
          could you eat that? How
                could you?

                    JULIE
               (snaps angrily)
          It's all your fault!

                    CURT
                   Me?

                                        87

                    JULIE
            You made me this way!

                    CURT
            I didn't make you do that!

                    JULIE
            Yes you did! You brought me
            back! You should've left me
                    dead!

                    CURT
            Is that what you want? You want
                to be dead?!

Julie just glares at him.

                CURT (cont'd)
            Well then I don't care... You're
            sickening the way you are now
            anyway... You're disgusting!

His words hit her hard. She suddenly
turns, runs off into the shadows. Curt
calls after her—

                CURT (cont'd)
                    Julie!

He follows her, searching the dark
viaduct.

                CURT (cont'd)
            Come on! Where are you?!

He sees something OFF SCREEN, then
darts OUT OF FRAME.

EXT. EDGE OF THE VIADUCT. NIGHT.

Julie is poised on the edge of the concrete railing, shivering, tears
streaming down her face. Curt
rushes up.

> CURT (cont'd)
> Julie...

EXT. LONG SHOT - BRIDGE. NIGHT.

Curt and Julie can be seen at the
railing of the viaduct.

EXT. EDGE OF THE VIADUCT. NIGHT.

Julie looks up at Curt. Curt starts toward her.

> CURT (cont'd)
> Look, you're being stupid, now
> come on!

He reaches out. She backs away
from him.

> CURT (cont'd)
> Get down from there!

She glowers at him.

89

                    JULIE
                     No...

                    CURT
        Damnit, don't screw around
     anymore! Now I mean it, get down!

                    JULIE
               Just go away...

                    CURT
                  Julie...

                    JULIE
                  Go away!

A beat. Curt's tone softens; he pleads
with her.

                    CURT
        Listen Julie... I didn't mean
          what I said... I'm sorry...

He steps closer to her.

                CURT (cont'd)
        All I want is for everything to
        be like before... that's all... I
         just want you like you were...
               like you used to be...

There is a long beat. Julie slowly
shakes her head; new tears well in her
eyes...

> JULIE
> But I can't be Curt... Don't you
> see? I can't be...

She suddenly turns away and leaps off
the ledge.

TIGHT ON CURT.

> CURT
> (screams, horrified)
> NO!

EXT. THE BRIDGE. NIGHT.

Julie plummets toward the raging river.
HIGH ANGLE OF RIVER. Julie SPLASHES
into the water and is swept away into
the darkness.
ON CURT. He rushes out of frame.

EXT. THE RIVER BANK - BY THE BRIDGE.
NIGHT.

A lean, wiry man bundled in ratty
clothes is watching from a storm drain
opening—He is RIVER MAN. He carries an
array of scavenged junk and a long
heavy stick.

ON CURT. He scrambles down a drain pipe
on the side of the bridge and takes off
down the river bank... River Man steps
INTO FRAME, starts to follow Curt.

CUT TO—

EXT. OUTSIDE THE DEAD END ALLEY. NIGHT.

Scratch's car drives by the police car
and the containment truck.

INT. SCRATCH'S CAR - TRAVELING. NIGHT.

Scratch takes a slug off a bottle of
bourbon as he drives along. Alicia is
next to him. Mogo and Felipe are in
back.

Music blasts on the radio.

                    SCRATCH
        Damn look at that... I never seen
          so many pigs turn out for one
                stinking little hit.

                    ALICIA
          Maybe it's what I thought,
        Santo... Maybe you killed that
                guy in the store.

                    SCRATCH
        I told you to relax about that. I
            didn't kill anybody. He was
                     alive.

Felipe yells over the music.

                    FELIPE

Santo, man I think there's
something wrong with Mogo!

Scratch turns down the radio, looks
into the rearview mirror.

                    SCRATCH
          What's the matter little bro?

                    MOGO
                  (shivering)
              I... I don't know...

                    FELIPE
              It's his arm. Look.

Felipe holds up Mogo's arm. Scratch
glances over his shoulder.

CLOSE ON HIS ARM. The small wound where
Julie bit him has started to fester.

Yellow and black streaks spread up and
down his arm.

                    SCRATCH
          Holy shit! What the fuck happened
                    Mogo?

                    MOGO
              She... she bit me...

                    SCRATCH
              Who bit you?

                    FELIPE
          That bitch in the store.

                    SCRATCH
     Shit... she gave you something...
     she gave you something bad...

                    MOGO
                  (panicky)
              Wha? what is it?

                    SCRATCH
     I don't know... gangrene...
     rabies... maybe that bitch had
                   rabies.

                    FELIPE
                  (recoils)
                  Rabies?!

                    ALICIA
          What're we gonna do?

                    SCRATCH
     What're we gonna do? I'll tell
     you what we're gonna do. We're
     gonna go find that bitch and make
              her pay for this!

                    FELIPE
     The only way out of that alley is
        through the sewer tunnel to the
           river bridge. Come on Santo,
           let's go down to the river.

CUT TO—

EXT. SIDE STREET BY ALLEY. NIGHT.

Scratch's car drives away, turns a
corner.

CUT TO—

EXT. L.A. RIVER - LONG SHOT. NIGHT.

Curt stumbles along the edge of the
dark river; River Man lurks behind him.

CURT
(calling desperately)
Julie!

She's nowhere in sight.

LOW ANGLE. Curt is heading away from
us. River Man's long stick looms into
the FOREGROUND, raises up and...
CLICK... CLICK... CLICK... It taps the
concrete.

TIGHT ON CURT. Curt wheels around,
startled.

CURT (cont'd)
What the hell do you want?!

River Man looks Curt over carefully.
After a moment, he finally responds...

                    RIVER MAN
                     (quietly)
          I saw a river swallow three men
           at once one time back in New
          Orleans. It was a night just like
                 this, pitch black...

There is a beat. Curt realizes the man
is probably just crazy. He turns and
starts away, urgently calls out—

                      CURT
                     Julie!

TRACKING ON RIVER MAN AND CURT. River
Man hurries up behind Curt.

                    RIVER MAN
           ...They were floating along just
           as nice as you please, then they
           round a corner and she rose up
           like a big ol' black viper and
           pulled 'em all under... just like
           that, swallowed 'em whole...
               never found one of 'em.

                      CURT
                     Julie!

                    RIVER MAN
           I saw it... I saw it all... just
             like I saw it this time...

Curt grows even more desperate, looking
frantically.

> CURT
> Julie! Damnit where the hell is
> she?!

EXT. RIVER ACCESS TUNNEL. NIGHT.

The headlights from Scratch's car
pierce the dark tunnel, coming toward
us. WE PAN with the car as it pulls out
onto the river bed.

EXT. L.A. RIVER. NIGHT.

TRACKING ON RIVER MAN AND CURT .Curt
leads the way, River Man still follows.
Curt is growing frantic.

> CURT (cont'd)
> Oh god where is she? where is
> she? (yells)
> Julie!

> RIVER MAN
> You know kid, from where I was it
> looked like she jumped in on
> purpose... It just might be that
> she doesn't want to be found.

> CURT
> (snaps angrily)

97

>   Why don't you mind your own
>   business!
>
>   RIVER MAN
>   I'm just telling you what I
>   saw...
>
>   CURT
>   Well no one asked you, all
>   right?!

Curt moves up into a CLOSE UP, suddenly
stops when he sees something.

>   CURT (cont'd)
>   Julie?

EXT. L.A. RIVER - A CEMENT ABUTMENT.
NIGHT.

A collection of brush, mud and debris
have collected against a cement abutment on the river bank. WE MOVE IN...

JULIE'S BODY can be partially seen
amidst the clutter, face down in the
water.

Curt rushes over, pulls Julie out of
the water, turns her over. She flops
limply onto his lap, soggy and bloated.

>   CURT (cont'd)
>   Julie honey... wake up...

River Man comes up behind Curt, looks
at Julie—she's obviously dead. He
slowly shakes his head.

> RIVER MAN
> Leave her be, kid... she's
> gone...

> CURT
> But she can't be!

Curt shakes her.

> RIVER MAN
> I'm tellin' you kid, they don't
> get any deader than that.

> CURT
> But you don't understand! It's
> impossible! She can't die!
> (frantically slaps her face)
> Julie!

Her eyes flutter open. She starts
COUGHING and GAGGING, water spills from
her mouth. Curt smiles, throws his arms
around her.

> CURT (cont'd)
> Oh thank God...

River Man stares, stunned—

> RIVER MAN

>   Mary mother of Christ...

Julie struggles weakly to get out of
Curt's arms as she CHOKES and spits up
more water.

>   JULIE
>   Let... let go of me!

>   CURT
>   No Julie.

>   JULIE
>   (frustrated)
>   Why are you doing this to me?
>   Why? why?

He holds her tighter, pats her gently,
comforts her.

>   CURT
>   Shhh... shhh... it's gonna be all
>   right...

She finally gives up, collapses helplessly into his arms.

>   JULIE
>   (desperate; scared)
>   Oh God Curt I... I don't know
>   what's happening to me... nothing
>   seems real anymore... sometimes I
>   don't even know where I am... I'm

> not alive but I'm not dead... God
> it's... it's so lonely...

Curt kisses her gently on the forehead.

                    CURT
> Julie honey, listen to me... if
> we stick together we can beat
>   this...

                    JULIE
>   No I... I can't...

                    CURT
> Yes... yes we can. Together we
> can... you just have to believe
> in us like I do... you can't give
> up on us... Julie you're all I've
> got... after the accident I
> realized that... you're all I've
> got and I don't ever want to let
>   you go... ever.

There is a beat. She slowly looks at
him, wanting to believe... The moment
is suddenly cut short by a BLINDING
LIGHT.

They all look over—

EXT. ACROSS THE RIVER. NIGHT.

SCRATCH'S CAR pulls up; the doors open.

101

Scratch and Felipe leap out. Scratch
points.

                    SCRATCH
              There they are!

EXT. BY THE ABUTMENT. NIGHT.

                    CURT
          What the hell do they want?

                    RIVER MAN
          Nothing good, that's for sure.

Curt helps Julie to her feet.

                    CURT
          Come on, we gotta get out of
                    here!

He looks around, not sure where to go.
River Man suddenly bolts away.

                    RIVER MAN
              Follow me!

EXT. STORM DRAIN OPENING. NIGHT.

River Man leads them into the dark
tunnel entrance.

INT. STORM DRAIN TUNNEL. NIGHT.

River Man, Curt and Julie head toward
us down the tunnel.

Scratch's car headlights shine into the
tunnel from behind them.

                              CUT TO—

EXT. STREET OUTSIDE DEAD END ALLEY.
NIGHT.

Reynolds and the Colonel wait by the
truck, listening to the police scanner.
Reynolds stares into the darkness,
whispers to himself.

                    REYNOLDS
     Damn you Curt... Where are you?

A beat. The Colonel lights a new cigar,
looks over at Reynolds.

                    COLONEL
     Come on John, try not to beat
        yourself up. We're doing
           everything we can...

The Squad Leader suddenly rushes up,
out of breath.

                    SQUAD LEADER
     Sir! We found their escape route!

Reynolds wheels around—

                    SQUAD LEADER (cont'd)
              It's a storm drain that leads
              from here to the viaduct under
                    the river bridge!

                         REYNOLDS
              Thank God! All right, radio all
              troops. Give them the twenty.

                       SQUAD LEADER
                         Yessir!

He goes to the truck, gets on the
radio and add-libs instructions... A
plain brown SEDAN suddenly screeches
up; the door pops open, Sinclair
climbs out. The Colonel eyes her sus-
piciously.

                         COLONEL
              What brings her down here?

Sinclair strides up, salutes.

                         SINCLAIR
              Sir, I just received this from
                     General Meade.

She hands the Colonel a FAX. The
Colonel reads it, then looks up at
Reynolds.

                         COLONEL
                      Son of a...

REYNOLDS
What is it?

SINCLAIR
(to Reynolds)
You are officially being relieved
of your command. I'm taking over
science operations effective
immediately.

Reynolds grabs the paper, reads it
over. Sinclair barks at the Squad
Leader.

SINCLAIR (cont'd)
Sergeant!

SQUAD LEADER
Yessir!

SINCLAIR
As of now I am in charge of this
situation. I want it upgraded
immediately to a total
indiscriminate containment.

REYNOLDS
(looks up, shocked)
A what?!

SQUAD LEADER
But sir the Colonel's son is—

SINCLAIR

There will be no discrimination
during containment. Do you
understand?

SQUAD LEADER
Yessir.

REYNOLDS
(yells angrily)
That's my son goddamnit!

COLONEL
John, calm down...

SINCLAIR
The odds are your son is probably
contaminated by now.

REYNOLDS
But there's still a chance!

SINCLAIR
A chance isn't good enough.

Reynolds reaches into the truck, grabs
the prototype rifle.

COLONEL
What the hell are you doing?
REYNOLDS I'm going to get my son.

SINCLAIR
Reynolds, you are no longer part
of this effort!

                    REYNOLDS
        Fine. I'll go as a civilian.

He rushes off. Sinclair yells
after him—

                    SINCLAIR
                    Reynolds!
                 (to the Colonel)
        He's violating my direct order!

                    COLONEL
        And if anyone asks me, I'll swear
            I never saw a thing.

                                        CUT TO—

INT. SEWER TUNNEL. NIGHT.

The sounds of MPs and POLICE can be
heard in the distance above. Curt has
his arm around Julie, helping her
along.

She grimaces, stretches her arm back
and forth; her joints CREAK and
CRACK.

                    CURT
        What's the matter, Julie?

                    JULIE
        I... I don't know, I got these
        cramps... I feel so stiff.

INT. OUTSIDE THE PUMP ROOM. NIGHT.

Gloomy and dank. Pale moonlight streams
in from grates overhead. River Man
leads them over to an old metal door
with no doorknob.

                    RIVER MAN
          It's okay, we're here...

River Man takes out a screw driver from
his pocket, jams it in the lock, twists
it. He pushes.the door open.

INT. PUMP ROOM. NIGHT.

A rusty -gray concrete room. Pipes and
ventilation ducts sprout in a tangled
maze from a series of large electric
pumps. Wisps of steam hiss from occa-
sional leaks, the motors hum...

                    RIVER MAN
          They'll never find you down here.

                    CURT
          Where are we?

                    RIVER MAN
          It's a pump room... I call it
                    home.

They help Julie over to a corner of the

room that has been set up as a living
space.

Tucked in and around the pipes is a
collection of PAINTINGS done on plywood
squares and SCULPTURE fashioned from
various junk that River Man has
collected.

They ease Julie onto a mattress in an
alcove; she shudders and shakes. River
Man feels her forehead.

> RIVER MAN (cont'd)
> Good lord, she's cold.

River Man grabs an old blanket, wraps
it around her.

> RIVER MAN (cont'd)
> Here. She'll be okay once she
> gets the chill of that river out
> of her.

> CURT
> Thanks...

Curt helps her take off her shoes.

> RIVER MAN
> What kind of trouble're you in,
> anyway?

Curt looks up at him, doesn't say anything.

                    RIVER MAN (cont'd)
          Come on kid, level with me. I may
          live with rats, but I'm sure as
                 hell not one of them.

                         CURT
                      (hesitates)
          We were on our way to Seattle but
          we got into a mess with those
          guys. There was an argument, a
                   guy was shot.

                      RIVER MAN
                   Did you do it?

                         CURT
          No they did, then they took off.

                      RIVER MAN
              So what're you gonna do in
                      Seattle?

                         CURT
          We hadn't really thought about it
          too much. I guess I'm going to
                 try and get a job or
          something... maybe get a gig
                 playing drums.

                      RIVER MAN
                 You're a musician?

CURT

Well I don't exactly know. I
haven't been in a group yet or
anything. But it's what I want to
try and do.

A beat. Curt smiles sardonically.

CURT (cont'd)
I know, it sounds stupid
doesn't it?

River Man thinks for a moment.

RIVER MAN
I don't think it sounds stupid at
all...

CURT
It doesn't? You don't think it's
crazy?

RIVER MAN
Hell no. Sounds like you got
something inside you, you just
gotta get out... Like me and my
painting.
I figure if everybody found out
what they got inside them and how
to get it out, there'd be a lot
more happy people...

CURT
(smiles)

You really think I can do
it, huh?

RIVER MAN
Sure, why not?
Of course what do I know? You're
talking to a guy who lives in the
sewers...

He starts to the door.

RIVER MAN (cont'd)
You two stay here and rest. I'll
keep a watch outside.

CURT
Hey...

River Man stops, turns back.

CURT (cont'd)
I don't even know your name.

RIVER MAN
So?

CURT
Well I just wanted to say
thanks... I guess I'll never be
able to repay you...

River Man thinks for a moment, then
reaches in his pocket and takes out a

silver Mardi Gras coin. He hands it to
Curt.

                    RIVER MAN
                    Here.

Curt takes the coin, looks it over.

                    CURT
               What's this?

                    RIVER MAN
          A Mardi Gras coin... Next time
       you find someone who needs help,
       just help 'em out. Then give them
       the coin and tell them to do the
       same for someone else. I figure
          as long as that coin keeps
       circulating, there'll be someone
       out there doing something good
                for somebody...

Curt puts the coin in his pocket,
smiles.

                    CURT
               You got a deal.

River Man continues to the door,
pauses, smiles.

                    RIVER MAN
          You can call me River Man...

113

He leaves.

OVER CURT'S SHOULDER, PUSH IN ON JULIE.
Julie is sitting on the edge of the
mattress, the blanket tossed aside. She
has pierced a couple of her earrings
through her lower lip and is rocking
back and forth, anxiously braiding a
strand of fabric into her hair.

Curt sits down next to her, gently
takes her twitching hand.

                    CURT
                  Julie?

She looks up anxiously.

                    JULIE
          Oh god Curt... what're we gonna
          do? what's gonna happen to us?

He kisses her gently.

                    CURT
          You know what's gonna happen to
                  us? We're gonna move to
          Seattle... We'll get a real nice
          place on the water. I'll get a
          gig in a band and you can hang
          out and party all night while you
                  watch me play...

Julie looks up at him hopefully.

                    JULIE
            Do you really think we'll
                  make it?

                    CURT
            Of course I do...

She manages a faint smile, kisses him.
Curt kisses her back. They embrace...
Julie's expression becomes blank;
there's a distance in her eyes. She
suddenly pushes away from him.

                CURT (cont'd)
            What's wrong?

She gets up, crosses the room. She is
confused, anxious.

                    JULIE
            Curt I... I can't do this
                  anymore...

                    CURT
                  What?

                    JULIE
            I can't keep pretending... I mean
            I want it to be like before but
              it isn't... I don't feel the
            same... I feel so... so goddamn
                  hungry!

                    CURT

> Come back to bed, please. It's
> gonna be all right.

                    JULIE
> Everything is not gonna be all
> right... I'm dead.

                    CURT
> Julie... I know that... but knowing
> that doesn't change anything...
> you're all I've got and I don't
> want to ever be without you...

She backs away, shakes her head.

                    JULIE
> This isn't about you... it's
> about me... I can't stand being
> like this.

She steps on something, suddenly
flinches.

                  JULIE (cont'd)
                    Ow!

CLOSE ON JULIE'S FOOT. A shard of GLASS
has pierced her heel.

                    CURT
> What's the matter?

Julie reaches down, grimacing in pain.

She slowly pulls the glass out of her
foot. A puzzled look crosses her
face...

She slowly takes the glass shard and
shoves it into the palm of her hand.
She inhales sharply, sensing the pain.

                    CURT (cont'd)
            What are you doing?

                    JULIE
              (quickly covering)
            Nothing... I... nothing...

She grimaces, digs the shard deeper.
She GASPS. A clarity flashes in her
eyes. She turns back to Curt, takes a
deep breath, manages a faint smile.

                    JULIE (cont'd)
            Curt I... I'm sorry... I just get
            confused sometimes.

She sits back onto the mattress with
him. He pulls her into his arms. She
suddenly GASPS, kisses him passionately. She is there with him now, completely in the moment...

CLOSE ON JULIE'S HAND. She clenches her
hand in a fist, digging the shard of
glass into her palm. A thin trickle of

117

thick, dark blood oozes out and drips down her wrist...

                    DISSOLVE TO:

INT. SEWER TUNNEL. NIGHT.

Scratch leads the way down the dark tunnel; Felipe is close on his heels. Alicia lags behind helping Mogo; he's in a cold sweat and he's pale. The wound on his arm has gotten worse.

                    MOGO
              (whispers shakily)
          I... I'm getting so cold...

                    ALICIA
          Santo, I think we should get Mogo
                to a hospital.

                    SCRATCH
          We will once we find the bitch.

                    ALICIA
          We're never gonna find our way
                out of here.

                    FELIPE
               (snaps angrily)
            Shut up, will you?

Scratch reaches a bend in the tunnel, peers off into the darkness.

                    SCRATCH
        Shit! They've got to be here
               someplace!

INT. STORM DRAIN OPENING. NIGHT.

Scratch's car's headlights stream into
the tunnel. Reynolds and the containment appear at the entrance. Reynolds
turns to one of the squad members.

                   REYNOLDS
        Radio in the license plate
        number of that car parked out
                   there.

The squad member nods. Reynolds looks
off into the darkness.

              REYNOLDS (cont'd)
        Let's try down here...

Reynolds leads the way into the tunnel.

INT. PUMP ROOM. NIGHT.

Curt's asleep—The mattress next to him
is empty. He rolls over, reaches out.
There is a beat, his eyes slowly open.

                    CURT
                  Julie?

He sits up, looks around.

CUT TO—

INT. ACCESS ROOM - A SERIES OF SHOTS.
NIGHT.

JULIE'S HANDS—She makes a fist around a
heavy rock and starts slowly wrapping a
leather strap around it, binding it
tightly into her palm...

HER CHEEK—A colorful shard of glass is
slowly pierce through the skin...

HER LEGS—She uses a shard of glass to
cut deep patterns and designs into her
skin...

HER ARM—Long rusty nails are shoved all
the way through her flesh...

HER NECK—An old rusty chain is laced
under her skin...

HER FINGER TIPS—Steel wire is pushed
through the ends forming claw-like ex-
tensions...

HER WRIST—An old pair of scissors are
shoved under the skin, along her wrist
and out her palm; a leather thong is
wrapped around it, securing it in
place...

INT. PUMP ROOM. NIGHT.

120

Curt gets out of bed, comes toward us
looking for Julie.

                    CURT (cont'd)
                    Julie?!

                                        CUT TO—

INT. SEWER TUNNEL - OUTSIDE THE PUMP
ROOM. NIGHT.

River Man is huddled against the wall,
fast asleep.

WE PAN AWAY, around a bend in the tunnel. Scratch slowly peers out of the
shadows. He turns to Felipe and
whispers.

                    SCRATCH
          The others can't be far...

                                        CUT TO—

INT. PUMP ROOM - BY THE ACCESS ROOM.
NIGHT.

Curt passes through a veil of escaping
steam and comes upon a small, dungeon-
like ACCESS ROOM.

WHAT HE SEES. Julie is on her haunches
in the shadowy doorway with her back to
him. She is doing something to her

face.

> CURT
> Julie?

She suddenly freezes.

> CURT (cont'd)
> What're you doing in there?

CLOSE TWO SHOT. She slowly lowers it to her side, REVEALING—The heavy rock that has been bound tightly to her hand.

Curt looks at the strange sight, curiously.

> CURT (cont'd)
> Julie what did you do to your hand?

There is a beat, she finally speaks quietly.

> JULIE
> I'm losing myself Curt... I... I
> don't know who I am...

> CURT
> What're you talking about?

She turns her head slightly into the half light. The pale light glints off something colorful on her cheek.

JULIE
It... it makes me feel real again
Curt... it makes me feel... alive...

Curt takes a step toward her, when suddenly—A TORTURED CRY echoes from outside. Curt freezes, looks around. The
CRY sounds again. Curt reaches down,
grabs an old length of pipe.

                    CURT (cont'd)
                Stay here.

He dashes away.

INT. SEWER TUNNEL - OUTSIDE THE PUMP
ROOM. NIGHT.

Scratch digs his knee into River Man's
back, pinning him face down on the edge
of the sewer stream.

                    SCRATCH
                Where is she?!

                    RIVER MAN
                I... I don't know...

Scratch plunges River Man's head into
the sludge. River Man coughs, gasps
for air.

                    SCRATCH

JOHN PENNEY

>   Don't lie to me, you crazy
>   bastard! Tell me where she is!

ON ALICIA AND MOGO. Felipe is in the
BACKGROUND prowling around the pump
room door, trying to get in. Alicia is
cradling Mogo in her lap.

His breathing is ragged, faint.

>   MOGO
>   (delirious)
>   Where? where am I? what's wrong
>   with me?

>   ALICIA
>   I don't think Mogo's gonna make
>   it unless we get him out of
>   here now!

>   SCRATCH
>   We will just as soon as he tells
>   us where the bitch is...
>   (to River Man)
>   Now spit it out!

River Man remains silent. Scratch dunks
him again.

ON FELIPE. He tugs at the crack in the
door jamb, trying to open it.

>   FELIPE

124

                    Come on, let's get this fucking
                              door open!

The door suddenly opens, REVEALING—Curt
on the other side, clutching the pipe.
Felipe steps back, startled.

                         FELIPE (cont'd)
                          Son of a...

Curt looks over at Scratch and River
Man, then back at Felipe. Felipe suddenly lunges at Curt, trying to grab
the pipe.

Curt takes a desperate, instinctive
swing—KAWHACK! The pipe SLAMS against
his forearm.
Curt approaches Scratch, brandishing the
pipe. Scratch shoves River Man's head in
the sludge, starts to get up—WHUMP! Curt
clubs him. Scratch doubles over.

Felipe leaps up behind Curt, tackles
him. They crash into the tunnel. The
pipe slips from Curt's hand.

Scratch gets up, takes out his pistol.
He shoves it against Curt's throat.

                          SCRATCH
                  Alright you little prick... let's
                  do this the easy way... Call her.

                        CURT
            What do want from us? We didn't
                    do anything...

River Man looks up, gasping for air.

                      RIVER MAN
            Leave the kid alone, he doesn't
                know where she went... she
                left... she's not here—

Felipe's boot suddenly enters frame—
KAWHUMP! He kicks River Man back.

                        FELIPE
                Shut up, loco pendejo!

ON CURT AND SCRATCH. CLICK! Scratch
cocks the hammer back.

                       SCRATCH
                Call her or I squeeze the
                        trigger!

                        CURT
            This is crazy... What did we do?

Scratch grimaces, his finger slowly
tightens around the trigger...

ON ALICIA AND MOGO. Alicia suddenly
calls out, shattering the stand-off—

                        ALICIA

Santo! Santo look!

She points to the door.

LOW ANGLE ON THE PUMP ROOM DOOR.

WE MOVE IN as JULIE emerges from the doorway into the shafts of light. The shards of GLASS pierced in her cheeks glint in the pale light. She slowly raises her arm that has been fortified with the long rusty NAILS and reveals the heavy ROCK dangling from her hand by the leather strap. The scissors in her other hand glimmer ominously...

She is strange and primitive, standing tall and menacing like some kind of ancient warrior.

MOVE IN ON CURT. He looks over at the new Julie. He whispers, stunned.

                    CURT
                  Julie?

WE PAN OVER... Scratch passes the pistol to Felipe.

                  SCRATCH
          If he moves, kill him.

                  FELIPE
                 (hisses)

                    Love to.

Scratch pulls out a knife as he steps
up to Julie.

                    SCRATCH
        So you wanna join the party, esa?

Julie remains silent. Scratch carefully
studies her face...

He steps closer, backing her against
the door jamb. He reaches out, stops
with his hands inches away from her
cheek. Julie recoils, revealing her
scissors hand. He continues, gently
touching the glass shards.

A twisted smile curls onto his lips.

                    SCRATCH (cont'd)
        I like it... I like it very
                    much...

He fondles the chain in her neck.

                    SCRATCH (cont'd)
        Kinky... very nice touch... you
        don't look like you've got rabies
        to me... you just look like my
                kind of bitch...

ON CURT AND FELIPE. Curt tries to
wrench away from Felipe—

                    CURT
              Leave her alone!

WHACK! Felipe SMASHES the pistol across
Curt's face. Curt crumples to the
ground.

                   FELIPE
          Don't tempt me, white boy...

Felipe steps on Curt's neck, pinning
him down.

Scratch grabs Julie, drags her into
shadows of the pump room doorway as she
kicks and fights. We HEAR Julie's
clothes being RIPPED.

River Man grimaces, climbs to his feet,
starts hobbling toward the door.

Felipe suddenly raises his pistol, aims
it at River Man—BOOM!—THWACK! The
bullet grazes River Man in the thigh.
He CRIES OUT, clutches his leg and
falls by the pump room door.

ON ALICIA AND MOGO. Mogo is fading fast
in Alicia's arms. She calls out.

                   ALICIA
          Santo! Mogo needs help!

Mogo suddenly clutches her desperately.

                                        129

                    MOGO
        Alicia... Alicia help me... don't
          let me die... don't let me—

He suddenly grimaces, his body shudders
and he slumps back in her arms. She
shakes him anxiously—

                    ALICIA
                Mogo? Mogo?

No response. WE PUSH IN on Mogo... His
lifeless eyes stare blankly back at
her. TILT BACK UP to Alicia—

                 ALICIA (cont'd)
               (yells anxiously)
                   Felipe!

ON FELIPE. He's not listening to her.
Scratch's beast-like GRUNTS grow louder
and louder, finally reaching a
crescendo; he CRIES OUT...

                    FELIPE
               Way to go Santo!

ON THE PUMP ROOM DOOR. Mid-way through
Scratch's guttural cry he is suddenly
cut off. Everything goes SILENT.

BACK ON FELIPE. He looks over, puzzled.

                 FELIPE (cont'd)

> Hey what'd you do? Go to sleep
> on her?

No answer. Alicia calls anxiously from
the BACKGROUND.

> ALICIA
> Mosco I think Mogo's dead!

She suddenly stops, looks over and
SEES...

ON THE PUMP ROOM DOOR. Julie emerges
from the dark doorway holding Scratch's
head by the jaw. His neck has been
hacked away, the only thing attaching
it to his body is the bloody vertebrae.
She raises her SCISSORS hand—They drip
with fresh blood.

ANGLE ON THE GROUP. Felipe steps off
Curt. Curt leans up. He stares, shocked
and sickened.

> CURT
> Oh my god Julie... what did
> you do?

Alicia SCREAMS. River Man looks up,
clutching his leg.

> RIVER MAN
> (horrified)
> Dear Lord...

ON JULIE. She dumps Scratch's body,
starts for Felipe.

REVERSE ANGLE. Julie approaches. Curt
dives out of the way.

> FELIPE
> Mo...ther...fuck...er...

TIGHT ON HER ROCK HAND. She jerks her
wrist. SWAP! The rock lands in her
palm.

TIGHT ON HER SCISSORS HAND. She raises
them, ready for battle.

ON FELIPE. He opens fire—BOOM! BOOM!
BOOM!

ON JULIE. The bullets punch into her
with no effect. She swings her rock
hand—WHACK! She BASHES Felipe in the
head with the rock.
Felipe falls forward. SHUNK! The scissors plunge into his stomach. Julie
BASHES the back of Felipe's head with
the rock.

WE MOVE IN... She hunches down, starts
feverishly gnawing on his neck and chin
as she repeatedly stabs the scissors
into his stomach.

ON ALICIA. She scrambles out from underneath Mogo's body, starts backing away.

                    ALICIA
              (screams hysterically)
              You crazy bitch!

ON JULIE. She slowly rises, looks over at Alicia. She drops Felipe's corpse.

Alicia clambers up the ladder on the wall. Julie reaches for Alicia.

CLOSE ON ALICIA'S SKIRT. Julie's razor finger nails shred Alicia's skirt and tear into her skin.

ON ALICIA. Alicia SCREAMS helplessly as Julie claws at her. CURT suddenly leaps up behind Julie, grabs her.

                    CURT
                  Stop it!

He pulls her away from Alicia.

                  CURT (cont'd)
              Damnit Julie no! No more!

WE MOVE IN... Julie looks at Curt—confusion and desperation in her eyes.

WE PUSH PAST THEM... Alicia slowly climbs down the ladder.

WE PAN with her as she starts to creep
away... She is almost home free, when A
HAND suddenly shoots up from the BOTTOM
OF FRAME, grabs her throat.

CRACK! MOGO bites her neck, pulls her
to the ground.

WE PUSH IN on Curt and Julie's reac-
tions. River Man yells at them from the
pump room door in the BACKGROUND.

                    RIVER MAN
            Kid get in here!

Julie is gazing at the carnage with a
disoriented, anxious look on her face.

                    CURT
            Julie! Come on!

He helps her over to the pump room door.

AT THE PUMP ROOM DOOR. Curt comes up
with Julie. River Man blocks their way.
He looks at Julie, then back to Curt.
Curt slowly shakes his head.

                    CURT (cont'd)
            I'm not going anywhere with
                out her!

The stand off is suddenly ended when—

Scratch's BLOODY HEAD suddenly rises up
in the FOREGROUND...

REVERSE ANGLE. They look back at
Scratch lurching toward them. He holds
a heavy length of pipe in his massive
hand; he snarls viciously as his head
jerks and twitches on the end of his
mangled vertebrae.

River Man suddenly steps aside.

                    RIVER MAN
                  Get in here!

They retreat into the pump room, SLAM
the door just as Scratch rushes up—
CLANG! He smashes the pipe against the
door.
                                    CUT TO—

INT. PUMP ROOM. NIGHT.

River Man stares at the door, stunned.

                  RIVER MAN (cont'd)
              Mary mother of Christ... loas...
                    the zombies...

CLANG... CLANG... CLANG... Repeated
blows from the other side begin to form
large dents in the old metal.

> **CURT**
> Shit! This isn't gonna hold 'em!

Curt grabs an old piece of wood from the rubble with a few nails in it. He places it across the door.

> **CURT (cont'd)**
> (to River Man)
> Help me with this!

River Man grabs a small sledge hammer, watches Julie warily.

> **CURT (cont'd)**
> (to Julie)
> Find some more nails!

Julie staggers away. River Man starts nailing the board into the old wood beams embedded in the cement around the door—KAWHUMP! The old metal door rattles on its hinges.

Scratch HOWLS outside. River Man turns to Curt.

> **RIVER MAN**
> What does it want?!

> **CURT**
> Us! He wants us!

Curt finishes hammering the board in place.

> CURT (cont'd)
> We need more nails...
> (calls out)
> Julie?!

INT. PUMP ROOM - IN FRONT OF THE ACCESS ROOM. NIGHT.

Curt rushes toward Julie.

> CURT (cont'd)
> Did you find anymore?

WE MOVE DOWN to Julie, hunched on the floor. She is binding her wrists together with an old extension cord. She looks up at him, a vacant look in her eyes...

> JULIE
> I... I'm losing myself, Curt...
> when I don't hurt, I get
> hungry... But the pain's not
> helping anymore...

Curt carefully takes her into his arms. She starts to drift away... Tears well in Curt's eyes.

WE PUSH IN... He clutches her close, whispers...

                    CURT
        It's all right... You're here
                with me now...

He rocks her gently in his arms.

                    JULIE
        Curt... I'm hungry again.

                    CURT
        Shhh... shhh...

WE PUSH IN TIGHT on Julie. She is
pressed up against him.

After a moment, her eyes glaze over,
she opens her mouth, bares her teeth...
Fear suddenly flashes in her eyes; she
pulls away from him, horrified.

                CURT (cont'd)
            What is it?

She holds her tied hands up to him.

                    JULIE
        Help me... You've got to tie
                me up!

Curt slowly shakes his head...

                JULIE (cont'd)
        Come on Curt! Don't you see

138

> what's happening to me?! I'm one
> of them!

                              SMASH CUT TO—

INT. PUMP ROOM - BY THE DOOR. NIGHT.

KABAAASH! The metal door CRASHES out-
ward off its hinges REVEALING Scratch,
Mogo, Felipe and Alicia—They SCREAM and
MOAN as they pound at the boards...

ON RIVER MAN. He stares in speechless
horror at the grotesque apparition
through the lattice work of boards.

THROUGH THE BOARDS OVER THE DOORWAY.

Scratch's hideous head suddenly BURSTS
through, snapping and snarling viciously.
Curt rushes up—KAWHUMP! He smashes the
pipe across Scratch's head. It
flies off.

ON SCRATCH'S HEAD KASPLAT! It lands in
acorner.

ON CURT. Curt shoves the end of his
pipe against the weakening boards,
leans into it with all his might.

                    CURT

>   I saw a ladder in that back room.
>   Where does it go?
>
>   RIVER MAN
>   Up to the street.
>
>   CURT
>   We don't have time!

Wisps of steam swirl from a weak weld
in the elbow joint of one of the pipes
above them.

River Man raises his hammer high over
his head. He brings it down with all
his might—CLANG! KAPOP! The pipe rup-
tures. WHOOOOOSH! Scalding steam
BLASTS out.

ON THE GANG. The steam slows the zombies down, but it's not enough to stop
them.

ON CURT AND RIVER MAN. Curt continues
to lean against the pipe through the
steam, holding the zombies out. River
Man yells over the deafening roar—

>   RIVER MAN
>   Damnit, it's not enough! You go
>   ahead, I'll stay and hold
>   them off!
>
>   CURT

What are you talking about? I'm
not gonna leave you here!

                    RIVER MAN
Kid, it's the only way!

                    CURT
Then you go! I still got two
good legs! I can get away
faster!

ON RIVER MAN'S LEG. He touches his
wound. In the background, WE SEE Mogo
reaching in under the steam.

BACK ON CURT AND RIVER MAN.

                    CURT (cont'd)
Now get going! I'll be right
behind you!

River Man exits frame. Curt looks over
his shoulder and sees Julie; he yells
at River Man.

                    CURT (cont'd)
Take her with you!

ON RIVER MAN AND JULIE. There is a
beat. River Man hesitates. Julie slowly
holds up her bound hands, looks at him,
pleading.

                    JULIE

141

     It's... it's okay... I won't hurt
                   you...

River Man scoops Julie into his arms,
carries her shaking body toward the access room as he mutters a prayer.

                   RIVER MAN
           Dear god, help us...

WE PUSH IN behind them, into the dark
access room.

BACK ON CURT. The steam is weakening.
Felipe lurches forward. Curt BASHES
him back with the pipe, turns to
run... WHUMP! Curt suddenly goes down.
WE FOLLOW him to the floor and
REVEAL—

Mogo. He's got Curt by the ankle. Curt
rears back his leg—TIGHT ON MOGO.

KAWHUMP! Curt kicks Mogo's blistery
face away from him.

BACK ON CURT. He scrambles to his feet
and dodges out of frame. The zombies
break through the boards, clamber in
after him.
Curt dashes into the shadows between
the massive pump motors. He crawls
along in the tight passage, looks back
and SEES—Felipe, Mogo and Alicia appear

behind him, reaching in, SCREECHING and
MOANING.

TIGHT ON CURT. He turns back, scrambles
deeper into the passage.

ON THE GANG. They clamber over each
other, trying to squeeze into the
narrow space between the pumps.

HAND HELD ON CURT. He creeps out from
behind the pumps and rushes into the
access room.

INT. ACCESS ROOM. NIGHT.

Curt SLAMS the door behind him, catches
his breath. WE MOVE IN... He looks up
into the shaft of light coming from
above.

                    CURT
              Julie? River Man?

UP ANGLE ON THE RUNGS IN THE WALL.

SHUNK... CRACK... SHUNK... CRACK... A
strange noise comes from the darkness
below. WE TILT DOWN, following the
shaft of light and REVEAL...

JULIE hunched over River Man's lifeless
body, feverishly digging his brains out
of his skull with her scissors.

JOHN PENNEY

Curt SCREAMS in horrified disbelief—

                    CURT (cont'd)
          My God no Julie... Not him!

CLOSE ON JULIE. She looks up at him,
trembling, blood streaming down her
chin. She has a wild, animalistic look
in her eyes—This isn't Julie anymore.
She has degenerated into someone else,
some thing else.

She SCREECHES in hideous torment,
lurches toward Curt.

ON CURT. He backs against the door, repulsed. CRACK! One of the zombie's
fists SMASHES a hole through the door
behind him, letting in a shaft of
light.

ON JULIE. She bears down on him.
BACK ON CURT. He raises the pipe.

                    CURT (cont'd)
          Julie stay back!

Julie lets out a blood curdling SCREAM,
leaps at Curt. He swings the pipe—
KAWHUMP! It SLAMS against her, knocking
her down. He raises the pipe to strike
again, but suddenly stops...

144

CLOSE ON JULIE. She looks up at him
with a pathetic, tragic sadness in her
eyes.

> JULIE
> (gasps raspily)
> Curt... help me... help me end
> this pain...

TIGHT ON CURT. Curt is paralyzed by a
sudden flood of remorse.

> CURT
> (whispers horrified)
> Oh God what have I done?

There is a beat, and then a look of
resignation crosses his face. WE TILT
DOWN... He slowly lowers the pipe, lets
it slip from his hand. It clangs to the
floor.
KABAASH! The zombies BURST through the
door, converge on Curt.

CLOSE ON CURT. He doesn't resist; he
has given up. Felipe bares his teeth,
about to bite Curt, when—KAPHOOMP!
THWACK! A bullet suddenly SLAMS into
the back of Felipe's head. The frost
and ice crystals spread over him.

He goes stiff, falls out of frame. WE
RACK FOCUS to the pump room behind him

and REVEAL—REYNOLDS wielding the para-
lyzing rifle. The rest of the squad is
behind him.

CLOSE ON REYNOLDS. KAPHOOMP! He fires
again.
REVERSE ANGLE ON ALICIA, MOGO AND CURT
Alicia turns and is hit in the forehead. WE PUSH IN TIGHT... Frost and ice
spread over her; she falls out of
frame. KAPHOOMP! THWACK! Mogo is hit in
the temple, freezes, and goes down too.

ON CURT. He looks out at his father,
surprised.

MOVE IN BEHIND CURT. Julie gets up,
reaching out for Curt.

> JULIE
> No Curt... don't... don't leave
> me...

OVER CURT'S SHOULDER OF JULIE. She
looks at him, pleading... Curt slowly
backs away from her.

EXTREME CLOSE UP. Reynolds raises the
barrel, aims straight at Julie—
KAPHOOMP! The blue bullet shoots out in
SLOW MOTION...

CLOSE ON JULIE. THWACK! She's struck in

the head. She arches her back,
twitches. The ice and frost suddenly
seize her up.

ON CURT. Julie's hand is outstretched
toward him as she goes down.

WE PUSH IN as Curt slowly backs up to
the wall. We continue in until we are
TIGHT ON CURT. He closes his eyes,
shutting out the world.

                              SLOW FADE OUt:

                              BLACKNESS...

                              FADE IN:

INT. RESEARCH CENTER - REYNOLDS' OF-
FICE. TWO DAYS LATER.

One of the drab green cubes. There are
moving cartons stacked all around. Curt
is slumped in a chair; he's cleaned up,
his hair is combed, he wears a new
button down shirt. He has a detached,
distant look on his face. His father
sits on the edge of his desk. The SOUND
has a muted quality; everything seems
soft, dream-like...

                    REYNOLDS
The Colonel told me you were very

> helpful during your debriefing.
> WE DRIFT around and pick up
>   Curt...

                    CURT
                  (shrugs)
         I just answered a lot of
         questions, that's all.

There is a moment of silence, Reynolds
gathers his thoughts.

                    REYNOLDS
         Curt, I just want you to know
         that I'm truly sorry about
         everything that happened.

Curt looks away.

                    CURT
         It's all right Dad.

A beat.

                    REYNOLDS
         You know when your mother died,
         the hardest thing I ever did was
         to let go... I just buried myself
         in this insane project and... and
         well because of that I know I
         haven't always been there for
                      you...

Reynolds moves into frame left, reaches out, gently touches his son's hand.

> REYNOLDS (cont'd)
> I thought I'd take a couple of weeks before Oklahoma City, we could spend time together, just the two of us... there's a lot we've got to talk about...

Reynolds pats Curt's shoulder.

> REYNOLDS (cont'd)
> Come on, let's get out of here.

Reynolds gets up.

> CURT
> Dad? what's gonna happen to Julie?

> REYNOLDS
> I really don't know... She's part of Sinclair's project now.

Reynolds starts to the door. Curt fol-lows. WE MOVE with them...

INT. CORRIDOR - OUTSIDE REYNOLDS' OF-FICE. DAY.

Curt and Reynolds come out of the of-fice and are met by the Colonel and

Sinclair. Sinclair appears to be comfortably in command.

> COLONEL
> John... Sinclair has requested
> that your report on the Walker
> girl be kept under wraps.

An agonizing SCREAM echoes from down the hall. Curt starts toward the sound; WE LEAD him down the hall, leaving Reynolds, the Colonel and Sinclair in the background...

> REYNOLDS
> But sir, the fact that we found
> her cognitive is significant. It
> proves that the living dead
> aren't just animated flesh. It
> proves they have an inner life...

> COLONEL
> That may be John, but—

> SINCLAIR
> (interrupts)
> The objective of this program is
> to create bio-weapons from these
> units, there's no point in
> confusing the issue. Now if
> you'll excuse me, I've got work
> to do.

She starts walking briskly TOWARD US.
The Colonel, looks at Reynolds apolo-
getically in the BACKGROUND.

                    COLONEL
        I'm sorry, John. I'm afraid we
        have to do what she says, we'll
        have to destroy your report...

Sinclair breezes into the lab where the
torturous SOUNDS are coming from.

INT. LABORATORY. NIGHT.

WE GLIDE behind Curt as he steps curiously into the laboratory.

A LAB TECH finishes closing the SLIDING
DOOR on the BARREL STORAGE ROOM as Curt
comes in.
Curt pauses and looks at the lab—Behind
an autopsy table are three cages that
run down the middle of the room. Curt
walks around behind the cages, WE TRACK
with him; the cages in the
foreground...

In each cage is a LIVING DEAD secured
by leather harnesses that run between
their legs and up over their shoulders.
Chains link the harnesses to wrist and
ankle bands, allowing very restrictive
movement. Steel balls have been secured

in their mouths. They writhe and twitch
in tortured agony.

Curt steps around the row of cages into
a CLOSE UP. He looks at the cage on
the end.
OVER CURT'S SHOULDER ON THE CAGE.

WE PUSH IN as the withered form slowly
looks up—It's JULIE. She is slumped in
the corner in a leather harness.

Her ornamentation has been removed,
leaving nothing but open wounds. She
trembles and quivers, IV tubes drip
sedatives into her.
A sign on the cage reads: "Specimen
#32, Brain Intact."

TIGHT ON CURT. He backs against the
plexiglas wall, stunned. The Lab Tech
steps up to him.

                    LAB TECH
          Pretty amazing, isn't it?

                    CURT
                  (startled)
                    Huh?

                    LAB TECH
          Believe it or not, you're looking
            at the weapons system of the
                    future...

CURT
The what?

An agonizing SCREAM suddenly comes from
the glass behind Curt. He spins around
and SEES—

INT. EXO ROOM.

RIVER MAN is inside a steel jointed exoskeletal frame.

Heavy steel rivets have been bolted
through the flesh of his arms and legs
in order to attach him to the metal
frame.

CLOSE ON RIVER MAN. SINCLAIR pushes an
electric drill through River Man's temple. He screams in agony. The drill bit
is removed and a metal frame is placed
over his head.

A stainless steel rod is placed against
the hole in his temple. An ASSISTANT
raises back a hammer, swings it
forward.

CRACK! The steel rod is driven clear
through River Man's temple, securing
him to the head brace. He SCREAMS, his
body jerks spasmodically.

WHIP TILT DOWN... His hand strains up-

ward, slightly moving the exoskeletal
frame.
Sinclair rushes over behind him.

SINCLAIR
Tighten the lock-off lever!

Sinclair pushes down a lock-off lever
on the back of the exoskeletal frame
with all her might.

River Man suddenly jerks backward as
the exoskeleton freezes up. The assistant comes over and helps Sinclair
who continues to struggle with the
lock-off lever.

INT. LABORATORY - BY THE CAGES. NIGHT.

Curt watches the torture, horrified.

LAB TECH
That one in there is the
prototype... (points to Julie)
This one's going next...

Curt looks over at Julie's cage.

CURT
You mean?

LAB TECH
That's right, they're all gonna
end up like that... bio

154

mechanical weapons driven by meat
batteries... never have to be fed
or recharged, they'll just keep
going and going...

Curt is flooded with pity and remorse.
He whispers to himself, horrified...

                    CURT
          My God no...

                  LAB TECH
          What'd you say?

Curt suddenly darts for Julie's cage.
The Lab Tech rushes up behind him.

              LAB TECH (cont'd)
          Hey!

Curt SLAMS the Lab Tech back—KAWHUMP!
He smashes against the plexiglas.

INT. EXO ROOM. NIGHT.

Sinclair and the Assistant look up,
letting go of the lock-off lever.

                  SINCLAIR
          What the hell is he doing in
          here?!

CLOSE ON THE LOCK-OFF LEVER. KATHUNG!
The lever snaps up.

ON RIVER MAN. He lets out a blood curdling SCREECH, swings back his steel
arms—KAWHUMP! His steel appendage
BASHES the Assistant who crumples over,
unconscious. WE MOVE IN TIGHT on
River Man.

He starts forward... River Man dashes
after him.

INT. LABORATORY - BY JULIE'S CAGE.

Curt is unhooking Julie from her harness; her eyes open groggily.

                    JULIE
              C... Curt?

                    CURT
      Don't worry Julie... it's... it's
      gonna be okay... I'm going to get
              you out of here...

ON RIVER MAN. He bursts into the lab
from the exo room, WAILING in pain.

The Lab Tech scrambles to his feet,
starts for Curt.

Sinclair rushes in, yells at the Lab
Tech—

                    SINCLAIR
              The gun! Get the gun!

156

Sinclair grabs the lock-off lever.
River Man wheels around, grabs her,
hurls her across the room. Sinclair
CRASHES to the floor by the cages. She
looks up, panicked, as River Man bears
down on her.

ON THE LAB TECH. He grabs a pump
shotgun off a rack on the wall. An
ALARM starts to blare. A steel containment door SLAMS shut, sealing
the lab.

ON CURT AND JULIE. Curt finishes un-
chaining Julie's harness. He helps her
out of the cage, takes off his jacket
and puts it around her. She looks up at
him groggily, a faint smile flickers
onto her face.

                    JULIE
     Oh god Curt... I... I knew you'd
               never leave me...

She weakly puts her arms around him,
they start toward the door.

ON THE LAB TECH. He brandishes the
shotgun, desperately trying to get a
clear shot of River Man who is pursuing
Sinclair behind the cages.

ON SINCLAIR. She yells desperately to
the Lab Tech—

                    SINCLAIR
              Shoot! Damnit shoot!

BOOM! The Lab Tech fires.

ON RIVER MAN. THWACK! River Man's arm
between his wrist and his shoulder is
BLOWN away. He is hurled against the
wall next to the circuit breaker box.
WE MOVE IN... River Man looks over at
his missing arm... His hand still
works.

ON SINCLAIR. She looks at the phe-
nomenon, surprised.

                    SINCLAIR (cont'd)
                 (yells to the Tech)
              Again! Hit him again!

BOOM! The Lab Tech fires again.

CLOSE ON THE CIRCUIT BREAKER BOX.
CALANG! The bullet punches into the box
—ZAP! It FIZZLES and SPARKS. The lights
go out. An ALARM echoes from outside in
the warehouse.
ON THE LAB TECH. He waits in the darkness, gun poised... CLANK! CLANK!

CLANK! We HEAR the sound of River Man's
heavy steel feet moving through the
lab... And then—CLUNK! Bright light
suddenly blasts in through the slats

REVEALING—River Man right on top of the
Lab Tech. He grabs the Lab Tech, hurls
him against the barrel storage room
door. WHUMP! His body SLAMS against the
door buttons. The shotgun flies from
his hands.

River Man starts pummels the Lab Tech
as the gate to the barrel storage room
starts to open behind them.

ON SINCLAIR. She grabs the shotgun.

BACK ON RIVER MAN AND THE LAB TECH
River Man heaves the barrels aside as
he pursues the Lab Tech. The barrels
CRASH to the floor—WHOOOSH... The mist
starts escaping from the broken seams.

WE PUSH IN... Through the swirling mist
WE SEE a HAND claw its way out of the
barrel.

ON RIVER MAN. He beats the Lab Tech unconscious just as Sinclair rushes in
with the shotgun.

BOOM! She fires. KATHWACK! The bullet
rips through River Man's leg. He looks
down—Part of his leg is missing.

LOW ANGLE MOVE IN. River Man stalks toward Sinclair. She backs into the barrels. He swings his mighty fist.

Sinclair dives out of the way at the last second—KABAASH! His hand smashes into a barrel.

WHOOOSH... The mist starts spewing out. Sinclair dives behind River Man, grabs the lock-off lever—THWUNK! She locks it off.
River Man suddenly jerks back, crashing into the barrels; they topple down, burying Sinclair.

ON CURT AND JULIE. They stumble through the misty lab toward the door. Several BARREL CORPSES loom out of the fog behind them. Curt tries desperately to open the door—It won't budge.

                    CURT
        Help us! Somebody let us out!

No luck. He spins around, looks behind him and SEES—The barrel corpses bearing down on him.

Curt quickly assesses his options then makes his move. He dashes over to River Man—CLUNK! He lifts the lock-off lever.

River Man suddenly lurches around, starts toward Curt. Curt stumbles back, panicked.

                 CURT (cont'd)

                    River Man! No!

River Man keeps coming. Curt frantically reaches into his pocket, takes
out the Mardi Gras coin.

                    CURT (cont'd)
          It's me River Man... Don't you
          remember? it's me...

CLOSE ON RIVER MAN. He suddenly hesitates... A glimmer of recognition
slowly appears in his eyes as he looks
at the coin. He suddenly lurches over,
grabs the containment door, pulls with
all his might. CRACK! ZAP!

The containment door sparks as it
opens.
River Man turns back, looks at Curt.
There is a beat.

                    CURT (cont'd)
          Thank you...

CLOSE ON RIVER MAN. He registers Curt's
gratitude... but the moment is suddenly
cut short—

ON SINCLAIR. She pops up, wielding the
shotgun—BOOM! BOOM! ON RIVER MAN
He is BLOWN against the wall.

ON SINCLAIR. She grimaces vindictively

as she moves in and aims the shotgun point blank at his head—BOOM! She delivers the final shot... There is a beat as she sneers triumphantly...

But her victorious moment is short lived—A BARREL CORPSE suddenly leaps up behind her—CARRUNCH! It sinks its teeth into her neck. She SCREAMS as it drags her down.

ON CURT AND JULIE. WE MOVE with them as they dart out of the lab, the other corpses lurching after them.

INT. CORRIDOR. NIGHT.

They rush down the hall, several barrel corpses in pursuit.

They dart around a corner.

ON CURT AND JULIE. They enter FRAME and pause, catching their breath.

Reynolds' VOICE suddenly echoes from OFF SCREEN.

                    REYNOLDS (O.S.)
                  Curt...

WE PUSH IN on Curt and Julie. Curt looks down the corridor.

CURT'S POV. A Barrel Corpse appears
from around a corner, coming toward
Curt and Julie.

ON CURT AND JULIE. Curt and Julie back
away... Another Barrel Corpse suddenly
jumps them from behind, tackles Curt—
CRACK! The corpse sinks its teeth into
Curt's arm. Curt CRIES OUT, knocks the
corpse away from him.
Curt and Julie dash away, turn a corner.

TRACKING WITH CURT AND JULIE. They rush
down a hall.

INT. CORRIDOR BY THE INCINERATOR ROOM.
NIGHT.

Reynolds has a fire extinguisher wedged
into the threshold of a containment
door, keeping it open. Curt and Julie
suddenly dash into FRAME and stop.

> REYNOLDS (cont'd)
> Curt! Curt hurry!

CLOSE ON REYNOLDS. He struggles to hold
the fire extinguisher in the opening as
the door strains to shut.

> REYNOLDS (cont'd)
> Come on Curt! Leave her... leave
> her and get out!

JOHN PENNEY

ON CURT. He looks down at Julie, shakes
his head.

                    CURT
            I… I can't dad…

                  REYNOLDS
      Damnit Curt! You belong out here!
         You don't belong in there
                  with her!

Curt remains frozen, clutching Julie
desperately. Reynolds pleads intently.

               REYNOLDS (cont'd)
      Curt... Curt please... You've got
        to let go... It's over... She's
                    dead!

There is a beat. Tears well in Curt's
eyes. He gasps, grimaces, looks down—

CLOSE ON CURT'S ARM. The bite has
started to turn yellow and black. WE
TILT UP... Curt looks back up at his
father, slowly shakes his head.

                    CURT
            (almost a whisper)
          I can't Dad... it's too
        late...it's too late for me...

Curt slowly backs away with Julie toward the INCINERATOR DOOR.

164

ON REYNOLDS. The fire extinguisher is beginning to buckle under the strain. Reynolds yells desperately for his son—

> REYNOLDS
> No Curt!

The Colonel rushes up behind Reynolds, grabs his arm.

> COLONEL
> John come on! We've got to get out before the whole building is sealed off!

> REYNOLDS
> CURT!!

> COLONEL
> Damnit John, come on!

The Colonel pulls Reynolds away. KAPOP! The containment door CRUSHES the fire extinguisher. WHOOOSH... CO2 spews out...

PUSH IN ON CURT AND JULIE. The mist swirls around Curt as he leads Julie into the incinerator room. WE CONTINUE TO MOVE with them through the door...

INT. INCINERATOR ROOM. NIGHT.

They step up to the incinerator.

Julie gazes up at him, disoriented.
He shudders, wipes his sweating
brow.

                    JULIE
          What? What's wrong Curt?..

Curt looks down, gently brushes the
hair from her eyes with his shaking
hand.

                    CURT
          I'm all right... everything's
                    fine...

Curt looks up at the chimney, a sign
reads: "Keep vent closed during disposal of contaminated materials."
THUNK!

He throws the lever on the flue so it
reads "OPEN."

                    JULIE
          Curt? We... we gotta get out...
          we gotta get out of here...

                    CURT
          We are Julie... we are...

He reaches over to the controls on the
oven.

INSERT ON THE FURNACE BUTTON. He pushes

the button—PHOOMPH! The flames
flicker on.

DOLLY IN ON CURT AND JULIE.

                    CURT (cont'd)
          We're getting out of here
                    together...

Curt helps Julie into the oven. She
looks at him distantly, confused...

                    JULIE
          Where? Where are we?

Curt kisses her tenderly, whispers.

                    CURT
          We're where we belong...

WE MOVE IN CLOSE ON THE LOVERS' LAST
EMBRACE...

They hold onto each other tight as the
yellow flames engulf their entwined
bodies...

                              DISSOLVE TO:

EXT. RESEARCH CENTER. DAY.

WE TILT UP the chimney from the research center... The black smoke bil-
lows up into the sky, rising higher and

higher until it blocks the sun... It
shimmers and sparkles with an eerie
metallic quality... It's beautiful...
It's Julie and Curt's ashes and...

They're alive.

                                SLOW FADE OUT:

                    THE END